Ramjanmabhoomi

Truth • Evidence • Faith

Other books by author

Ramjanmabhoomi

Truth • Evidence • Faith

Arun Anand
Vinay Nalwa

Published by
PRABHAT PRAKASHAN PVT. LTD.
4/19 Asaf Ali Road,
New Delhi-110 002 (INDIA)
e-mail: prabhatbooks@gmail.com

ISBN 978-93-90315-54-3
RAMJANMABHOOMI
by Arun Anand and Vinay Nalwa

Edition
2025

Price
₹ 350.00 (Rupees Three Hundred Fifty only)

Printed at
Narula Printers, Delhi

For

Dhananjay

Preface

The issue of building a Ram Temple at Ayodhya in the state of Uttar Pradesh has dominated the Indian polity as well as public discourse over the last four decades. There have been several books written on this issue. But that, ironically, is a problem too as arguments and rhetoric have dominated the facts in this case.

As the debate which raged on this issue pushed the facts to the backseat with ideologies occupying the driving seat, the result was that those who were born in India after 1992, when the disputed structure, often called Babari mosque also, was demolished by Kar Sevaks in Ayodhya, couldn't fathom the importance of 'Ramjanmabhoomi'.

Thus we often heard the arguments in our drawing rooms and in debates in colleges and schools that why shouldn't we build a school or hospital instead of a temple at the birthplace of Lord Rama. Those who put forward such arguments shouldn't be blamed as most of the content they read or watched was full of passionate arguments from the supporters as well as opponents of Ram Temple. There was hardly anyone who could dispassionately put forward the facts and let the readers or viewers decide to form an informed opinion.

This book has been written precisely to fill up this gap. We have traced this interesting journey right from the birth of Lord Rama upto the Supreme Court's final verdict on this issue that paved the way for building a Ram Temple at the birth place of Lord Rama. We have tried to do our best to check facts and cross reference them. However, your feedback is always welcome.

We would like to acknowledge the immense support we received from prominent advocates Shri Aman Sinha, Shri Virag Gupta and Shri Rajesh Gogna. We also want to thank the editorial and the design team at Prabhat Prakashan.

Most importantly we want to express our gratitude to our readers for taking out time to read this book. We are looking forward to your feedback.

—Arun Anand
Dr. Vinay Nalwa

Contents

1

Rama and *Ramayana*

Rama and *Ramayana* are inseparable parts of the Hindu culture and Bharat. However, in the middle of 1980s, when a movement was launched to rebuild the temple of Lord Rama at Ayodhya, a section of historians and intelligentsia raised doubts on even the existence of Lord Rama.

In ancient Indian literature, *Ramayana* is one of the most significant milestones and continues to be a spiritual beacon several centuries later. This monumental work, which depicts the life and times of Lord Rama, had great influence on Bharatiya culture and values. Its renditions are not restricted to one religion, one nation or one time-period. It unites Indian culture with South-east Asian countries, like Thailand, Cambodia, Indonesia, Laos, Myanmar and Nepal. It has also made its presence felt in Singapore, Malaysia and Vietnam.

Ramayana is the life story of Lord Rama, the seventh incarnation and the perfect *avatar* of the Supreme Protector Lord Vishnu. The symbol of courtesy and virtue, who held high moral values and has always been most revered among the Hindu deities, Rama has been widely accepted as a historical figure – an ideal king of ancient India – who took birth on the earth to destroy the evil forces.

Rama is a beautiful amalgamation of earthly and divine. Allthrough his life, Rama not only remained noble, generous and fearless, but also a very kind and considerate king to his people. A number of scholars, who have worked on the age and times of Lord Rama, broadly agree that through his life of holy compliance with purity, simplicity and self-sacrifice, renunciation like a divinity, he has been a guiding spirit for the society on morality, values and how to be spiritually aligned while carrying on duties of the world.

When we talk about the highly held virtues of Hindu *Dharma* we see the personification of all in Lord Rama. He was a noble, generous, fearless, kind and considerate king to his people

Sage Valmiki, was the first to recite the story of Rama. Later it became a way of life for the people who revered the *Ramayana's* main character. In the words of Maurice Winternitz who published his famous work, *A History of Indian Literature* in three volumes in 1920s and 1930s, "It has become the property of the entire Indian folk and – as perhaps no other poem in entire world literature – has influenced the whole thinking and writing of the folk through all centuries... since more than 2,000 years the poem of Rama has remained alive in India and it continues."

Hindu civilisation is an exceptional blend of believers and non-believers. There have been astronomers, historians, archaeologists and foreign travellers who have identified and clearly corroborated the dates, incidents and geographical places that have been mentioned in Valmiki's *Ramayana* and there are also others who question the existence of Rama as a historical figure. For some historians, Rama is just a central character of a well-written story based on myth and then there are historians who through scientific research have repeatedly proved Rama's existence.

While mythology may have supernatural events and beings, an epic narrates events and occurrences that are actually part of history. Not only the historians of the East but many experts from the West have also successfully corroborated the dates of Rama's life. They have also identified the places associated with him. Dismissing the contention that *Ramayana* is only a literary piece, Ralph T.H. Griffith who had translated Valmiki's *Ramayana (The Ramayana of Válmíki,* 1895 asks, "How could an epic so dear in India to the memory of the people, so deeply rooted for many centuries in the minds of all, so propagated and diffused through all the dialects and languages of those regions, which had become the source of many dramas, which are still represented in India, which is itself represented with such magnificence, year after year and to such crowds of people in the neighbourhood of Ayodhya, a poem which at its very birth was welcomed with such fervour as the legend relates that the recitation of it by the first wandering rhapsodists, has consecrated and made famous all the places visited by them and where Rama made a longer or shorter stay, how I ask, could such an epic have been purely allegorical?"

Gasper Gorressio (1808-1891), an Italian Indologist who, like Griffith, translated Valmiki's *Ramayana* thinks that some events must have happened in the distant past, the memory of which has so impressed itself indelibly on the fancies of the Hindus that there is no possibility of the story ever dying until some geological alterations of the features of the country come to pass.

F.E. Pargitter observed in *The Geography of Rama's Exile* (1894), "The geographical knowledge revealed in the epic could hardly have been obtained except by actual visit to these places by some persons."

Swami Vivekananda said, "This the great ancient epic of India. Rama and Sita are ideals of the Indian nation. When you study its characters, you can at once find out how different is the ideal in India from that of the West. There is no other *Pauranika* story that has so permeated the whole nation, so entered into its very life and has so tingled in every drop of blood of the race."

In the year 1973, in the All India Seminar on *Ramayana* held at Thiruvananthapuram, a book on *Sri Rama Patha Yathirai* was brought out by V.D. Ramswami. The book contains maps describing his trek in the forests and also all the places visited by Rama during his life.

Historian Nandita Krishnan has observed that the *Ramayana*'s geographically correctness with each and every site on Rama's route cannot only be easily identified with all its continuing traditions, but there are temples to commemorate Rama's visit. How can a writer of about 1000 B.C. have the means to travel around the country to formulate a story, fitting it into local folklore and building temples for greater credibility? Explaining the importance of these holy sites, Krishnan says, "All the places visited by Rama, still retain memories of his visit as if it happened yesterday. Time, in India, is relative. Some places have commemorative temples; others commemorate the visit in local folklore. But all agree that Rama was going from or to Ayodhya. Why doubt connections when literature, archaeology and local tradition meet? Why doubt the connection between Adam's Bridge and Rama, when nobody else in Indian history has claimed its construction? Why doubt that Rama travelled through Dandakaranya or Kishkinda, where local non-Vedic tribes still narrate tales of Rama? Why doubt that he was born in and ruled over Ayodhya?"

"Rama's memory lives on because of his extraordinary life and his reign, which was obviously a period of great peace and prosperity, making *Ramarajya* (rule of Rama) a reference point. People only remember the very good or the very bad."

Noted writer and researcher on Hinduism, Stephen Knapp gives a detailed account about historicity of Rama in an article titled, *Lord Rama: Fact or Fiction.*

Knapp says, "Valmiki, who wrote the *Ramayana*, was a contemporary of Rama. While narrating the events of the epic, he has mentioned the position of the planets at several places."

Quoting Pushkar Bhatnagar, author of the book *Dating the Era of Lord Rama*, Knapp says, "He (Bhatnagar) explains that by using recent planetary software, it is possible to verify that these planetary positions actually took place precisely as specified in the *Ramayana*. These were not just stray events, but the entire sequence of the planetary positions as described by Valmiki at various stages of Rama's life which can be conveniently verified today as having taken place."

Bhatnagar further explains, "This information is significant, since these configurations do not repeat for lakhs of years and cannot be manipulated or imagined so accurately, without the help of sophisticated software. The inference that one can draw is that someone was present there to witness the actual happening of these configurations, which got recorded in the story of Rama."

Bhatnagar provides the following quote from the *Ramayana*: "Rama was born on the *Navami tithi* of *Shukla Paksha* of *Chaitra masa* (9th day of the increasing phase of the moon in the lunar month of *Chaitra*]. At that time, the *nakshatra* was Punarvasu, and Sun, Mars, Saturn, Jupiter and Venus were in Aries, Capricorn, Libra, Cancer and Pisces respectively. *Lagna* was Cancer and Jupiter and Moon were shining together"(*Ramayana 1.18.8,9*).

The conditions can be summarised as follows, according to Bhatnagar:

1. Sun in Aries
2. Saturn in Libra
3. Jupiter in Cancer
4. Venus in Pisces
5. Mars in Capricorn
6. Lunar month of *Chaitra*

7. 9th day after New Moon (Navami *Tithi, Shukla Paksha*)
8. Moon near *Punarvasu nakshatra* (Pollux star in Gemini constellation)
9. Cancer as *lagna* (Cancer constellation rising in the east)
10. Jupiter above the horizon

Bhatnagar explains, "By using a powerful planetarium software, I found that the planetary positions mentioned in the *Ramayana* for the date of birth of Lord Rama had occurred in the sky at around 12.30 p.m. of 10th January 5114 B.C. It was the ninth day of the *Shukla Paksha* of *Chaitra* month too. Moving forward, after 25 years of the birth of Lord Rama, the position of planets in the sky tallies with their description in *Ramayana*. Again, on the *amavasya* (new moon) of the 10th month of the 13th year of exile, the solar eclipse had indeed occurred and the particular arrangement of planets in the sky was visible. (Date comes to 7th October, 5077 B.C.). Even the occurrence of subsequent two eclipses also tallies with the respective description in Valmiki's *Ramayana*. (Date of Hanuman meeting Sita at Lanka was 12th September, 5076 B.C.). In this manner the entire sequence of the planetary positions gets verified and all the dates can be precisely determined."

Although this provides verification of the existence of Lord Rama according to calculations as given in the *Ramayana*, some people feel the timing for the day and year of his birth may be different than what the planetarium software indicates. For example, Vedic astrologer Nartaka Gopala Devi Dasi points out, "Regarding the calculation of Lord Rama's birth as 10th of January 5114 B.C.E.—birthday of Rama, observation at 12.30 p.m., there are two reasons why this cannot be correct. His rising sign, or *lagna*, is Cancer. That places Aries in the tenth house, and he has the Sun in Aries. The placement of the Sun in any birth chart will tell the time of day of the birth. Sun in the tenth house means birth at noontime (approx. 11 a.m. to 2 p.m.). There are no exceptions to this. (Lord Krishna appeared at midnight, the Sun is in Leo, 4th house for Taurus rising. Birth at 6 p.m. means seventh house of Sun. Birth at sunrise means first house of Sun.) Also, in Lord Rama's chart the Sun is in Aries, and the dates for Sun in Aries are fixed, which means the same each year on April 14th to May 13th. So how did the January 10 date come up? These two *jyotish* corrections are common sense that any Vedic astrologer would immediately see." So there may be a difference in what the planetarium software suggests. This also corroborates why we, who follow the Vedic calendar, celebrate Lord Rama's appearance in April-May each year. So the traditional date appears accurate."

According to Meenakshi Jain (*Rama and Ayodhya*), "The *Ramayana* seemed to have originated in the Kosala region, ruled by the Ishvakus in Ayodhya. Ayodhya court bards (*suta*) must have recounted the travails of Rama. From these tales, Valmiki, whose hermitage was situated on the bank of the Ganga, prepared a single homogenous production. This was learnt by professional rhapsodists, who recited it to the public in their wanderings through the country."

"There were over twenty-five renditions of *Ramayana* in Sanskrit alone, and many more in the vernaculars. Father Camille Bulke counted three hundred tellings. However, Valmiki's account was always the most popular and most widely accepted. It is also widely recognised as the earliest surviving version of the Rama story."

Ramayana Beyond India

"As early as A.D. 251, K'ang-seng-hui rendered the Jataka form of the *Ramayana* into Chinese and, in A.D. 472, another Chinese translation was prepared of the *Nidana* of *Dashratha Jataka* from a lost Sanskrit text, by Kekaya. In the sixth-century, the Simhala poet-king, Kumaradasa, composed the *Janakiharana*, the earliest Sanskrit work of Ceylon. In seventh century Cambodia, Khmer citation attested to the popularity of the *Ramayana*. An inscription declared that a certain Somasharman presented 'the *Ramayana*, the *Purana* and the complete Bharata to a temple. Towards the close of the ninth century, an east Iranian version of the *Ramayana* appeared in Khotanese, an Iranian dialect. The story of Rama spread in the northernmost lands of Asia from Tibet, where it was found in two versions in manuscripts of the seventh-ninth centuries. The oldest manuscript of the *Ramayana* of Valmiki, dated A.D. 1075, is preserved in Nepal," says Jain.

She further adds, "The *Ramayana* was translated and adapted into several European languages. During 1806-1810, the Baptist missionaries, William Carey and Joshua Marshman translated the first two books... In 1808, Friedrich Schlegel presented a partial translation in German, in his *On the Languages and Wisdom of Indians.* In 1829, his brother, August Wilhelm Von Schlegel prepared an incomplete translation in Latin. The first complete translation was the five-volume rendition into Italian by Gaspare Gorresio, between 1847 and 1858. Almost at the same time came a nine-volume rendering in French by H. Fauche between 1847 and 1858; and a five-volume presentation in English by Ralph T.H Griffith between 1870 and 1874.

"The Rama story occurred in three early Budhist texts—the *Dasharath Kathanam*, the *Anamakam Jatakam* and the *Dashrath Jataka*. The *Dasharath Kathanam*, the earliest, belongs to the first-second century A.D.," says Jain.

About historicity of Lord Rama, Kunal Kishore says in *Ayodhya: Beyond Adduced Evidence*, "Rama was born in the dynasty of Ikshvakus, the son of Manu and the grandson of Vivasvan, i.e. Surya (Sun). Valmiki, the first poet (*adikavi*),wrote the narrative of this dynasty, i.e. the *Ramayana*.

Rama was an ideal son
an ideal husband
an ideal brother
an ideal king &
a self discipline all-sacrificing worldly yet ascetic.

"Since Valmiki wrote great events of the dynasty, the *Ramayana* has remained the most popular scripture and Rama is the most popular deity with Ayodhya being as the most sacred place for millions and billions of his devotees. This uninterrupted command of absolute reverence to the supreme God and the holy city entitles Ayodhya to a unique position which makes it an essential part of Hinduism and the Ramjanmabhoomi inalienable forever.

It is written in the Valmiki *Ramayana* that God requested Vishnu to take birth, in the interest of the people, in the house of Dashrath, the king of Ayodhya, Lord Vishnu, before taking incarnation, decided his birth-site.

"It is well known that Kaushalya gave birth to Rama who has been called Jagannath. It was not the birth of an ordinary man. Ayodhya was blessed with the arrival of the Lord of the whole world. Even then some historians say that Ayodhya was never sacrosanct because of the birth of Rama.

"In the Valmiki *Ramayana*, there is a reference to temples and Gods whom Rama used to worship. When Rama was ready to start his journey for *vanvasa* (exile in forest), Kaushalya took him to the temples and gods whom Rama used to worship.

"In *Mahabharata,* Vyasa calls Rama as *rashtrapati,* i.e. the master of the nation. Vyasa predicts in the *Mahabharata* that so long as the earth is in existence, gods and all the people including *asuras, gandharvas, yakshas, rakshasas* will sing the saga of Rama."

***Ramayana* in South**

According to Kunal Kishore (*Ayodhya: Beyond Adduced*

Evidence), "Rama's story is found in the earliest phase of the Tamil literature, i.e. the Sangam literature in the beginning of the Christian era. Purananuru mentions the abduction of Sita, Ahananuru refers to Rama holding a meeting on the sea-coast before attacking Lanka and Paripadal has many episodes from *Ramayana*. *Ramayana*'s references have been seen in the famous works of Sangam epics, *Silappadhikaram* and *Manimekhlai*.

"However, the most outstanding epic written in Tamil on Rama saga was by the great poet Kamban whose date has been assigned from 9th to 12th century by various critics. According to one tradition, it was composed in 9th century and placed in Ranganatha temple and according to another, this Tamil *Ramayana* or *Ramavataram* was composed in 12th century. And it was placed before scholars of Madurai in famous Madurai temple. It attained unprecedented popularity and like Tulsidasa's *Ramcharitmanas* in north India, became popular in every Tamil house. And it has been a source of inspiration for millions of Tamils. Kamban's *Ramavataram* confirms both the popularity and divinity of Rama in ancient India in the land distant from India.

"In Telugu language, Rama's story was so popular that several *Ramayana*s were written with the result that in Andhra Pradesh, there is not a single important village which does not have a Rama temple. Ramanavami is celebrated throughout Andhra Pradesh with much enthusiasm. Out of a number of works on the *Ramayana*, four are very important. They are *Ranganath Ramayana*, *Bhaskara Ramayana*, *Molla Ramayana* and *Katta Varadarayu Ramayana*. *Ranganath Ramayana* also has a story of the squirrel helping in the construction of the bridge over the sea and Rama's appreciation of its splendid devotion is well known throughout the country. *Ranganath Ramayana* is a complete *Ramayana* which contains 17,290 indegenious *dvipad,* i.e 34,580 lines and was written about 335 years before the composition of *Ramcharitmanas* by Tulsidas."

To conclude, it is a widely accepted fact that for Hindus, Lord Rama has always been a role model in every sphere of individual and social life. Millions of people feel the reciprocation whenever they devote themselves to reading or hearing the *Ramayana* (even in its different versions or translations) when they go to the temples dedicated to Rama since ages this devotion & reverence guides/motivates all to be as virtuous as Rama..

□

2

Ramjanmabhoomi and Ayodhya

For crores of Hindus, Ayodhya, a town situated in the Indian state of Uttar Pradesh, has always been the place where Lord Rama was born as mentioned in Valmiki's *Ramayana*. Ayodhya literally means 'unconquerable'. Ayodhya, for Hindus, is the gateway to heaven and is considered as immortal as Rama.

Ancient Indian scriptures mention the importance of Ayodhya in several texts. *Garuda Purana*, an ancient Indian scripture on Vaishnavism, says:

Ayodhyā Mathurā Māyā Kāsi Kāñchī Avantikā ।
Purī Dvārāvatī chaiva saptaitā moksadāyikāh ॥

—*Garuda Purana* I XVI. 14

The *Garuda Purana* says in this verse that there are seven places where one can attain *moksha* (salvation). They are Ayodhya, Mathura, Māyā, Kāsi, Kāñchī, Avantikā and Dvārāvatī.

In all the versions of *Ramayana* cutting across languages and geography, Ayodhya has been mentioned as the place where Lord Rama was born.

There is evidence of reverence since time immemorial for Ayodhya and Lord Rama. Ayodhya Mahatamya and Vishnu-Hari inscriptions are two important sources of information in this regard. Kishore Kunal has reproduced some of the important verses in this context in *Ayodhya Revisited*.

Ayodhya Mahatmya of Rudra-yamala

(Rudra-yamala is mentioned in a manuscript of the Brahma-yamala dated 1052 A.D.)

सरयूतीरपूतानां जन्मभूम्याः विलोकिनाम्।
दर्शनात् पातकं तेषां कल्पकोटिशतायुतान्॥ 35 ॥

(All sins of those persons, who, after being purified on the Saryu's bank, visit the *Janmabhoomi*, are effaced, by its mere glimpse, for hundred, thousands and crores *kalpas*.)

राममन्दिरमासाद्य दर्शनं क्रियते नरैः।
मनसापि स्मृतं येन मुच्यते चरणत्रयात्॥ 36 ॥

(Having reached the temple of Rama, men, who have his *darsana* or even his remembrance, are liberated from the *charana-trayam*, i.e. birth, life and death.)

दर्शनं जन्मभूमेश्च स्मरणं रामनामतः।
मज्जनं सरयूतीरे कृतं वै पापनाशनम्॥ 37 ॥

(By the *darsana* of the *Janmabhoomi* or remembrance of the name of Rama or bathing in the *Saryu* river, all sins are destroyed.)

अयोध्यानगरं पुण्यं स्मृतं वै पापनाशनम्।
धान्यं यशस्यमायुष्यं पुण्यं पापहरं फलम्॥ 38 ॥

He, who remembers the city of Ayodhya, is blessed with wealth, reputation, long life, virtues and destruction of sins. (quoted from the twelfth chapter of the *Ayodhya–mahatmya* manuscript of the Rudra yamala, dated 180.)

Vishnu-Hari Inscription

This inscription was discovered from the debris of Babri mosque after it was brought down in 1992.

Verse 5

वंश्यन्तदेव कुलमाकुलतानिवृत्तिनिवर्यूढमप्रतिम (विक्रम) जन्मभूमिः।
यत्रातिसाहससहस्रसमद्धिमा मा नो जनिष्ट जगदिष्टतमोत्तमश्रीः॥

(It is the abode of the dynasty which had succeeded in ending all anxieties and is the birthplace of a man with unmatched valour, i.e. Rama. Herein resides the person who is illuminated with the power of thousands of valorous deeds, i.e. Rama. He may not generate greed in us even for the most precious wealth hankered after by the world.)

Verse 21

टंकोत्खातविशालशैलशिखर श्रेणीशिलासंहति-
व्यूहैर्विष्णुहरेर्हिरण्यकलशश्रीसुन्दरं मन्दिरम्।
पूवर्वैरप्यकृतं नृपतिभिर्येनेदमित्यद्भुतं
संसारावर्णवशीघ्रलंघनपघूपायान्धिया ध्यायता॥

(He, contemplating a shortcut to cross the ocean of the world, made this beautiful Vishnu-Hari temple adorned with a gold *kalasa* (urn), on a scale never done before by any preceding king. It was constructed with the rocks sculpted out with chisels from the mountain peaks.)

उद्दामसौधविबुधालयनीमयोध्यामध्यास्य तेन नयनिन्हुत वैशसेन।
याकेतमण्डालखण्डमकारि कूपवापीतप्रतिश्रय तडागसहस्रमिश्रम्॥

(By residing at Ayodhya which was full of towering abodes and temples, he, who was the embodiment of righteous conduct, constructed thousands of wells and tanks, rest houses and ponds throughout the *Saketamandala*.)

Besides this ancient Indian text on Ramjanmabhoomi, we get a clear and precise description of Ayodhya and the place where Lord Rama was born in accounts of many foreign travellers', archaeologists' and scholars' accounts, which are elaborately described.

William Finch, the European traveller (1608-11), who visited Ayodhya, has written in his travel account about the existence of the ruins of Ramkot, the castle of Ramachandra and houses where Lord Rama had incarnated thousands of years ago.

Finch recorded that Rama was born in the human form to see the *tamasha* (theatrics) of the world. He further writes that the castle was built four hundred years ago. He did not see any mosque in the area but saw a lot of Brahmins and Hindu pilgrims. He found Brahmin priests in the ruins of the castle, recording the names of pilgrims. He was told it had been a custom for the last several hundred years. Finch informs that Ayodhya is a city of ancient note. Regarding the castle of Ramachandra, he may have been referring to the temple of Rama. The presence of Brahmins in the ruins confirms that it was a temple and the entire surrounding area was controlled by the Hindus.

William Finch's travel account clearly establishes the existence of the birthplace of Lord Rama.

Kishore Kunal has mentioned Joannes de Laet's account of Ayodhya in *Ayodhya Revisited*. Joannes was an author, geographer, philologist and naturalist. He was also one of the directors of the Dutch East India Company. He wrote a book, *De Imperio Magni Mogolis Sive India Vera Commentaries* about Ayodhya in 1631 in Latin. The book was translated into English by John S. Hoyland. The English translation was published in 1927 in Patiala. Following is an excerpt from Joannes' book's first chapter in which Ayodhya is described as:

"Thence (from lucknow) to Oudee (an ancient city, once the seat of Pathan kings, but now almost deserted) 50 *cos* (*kos* – a unit used to measure distance between two places primarily in northern India). Not far from this city may be seen the ruins of the fort and palace of Ramachand, whom the Indians regard as God most high: they say that he took on human flesh so that he might see the great *tamasha* of the world. Amongst these ruins live certain Brahmenes (Brahmins) who carefully note down the name of all such pilgrims as duly perform their ceremonial ablutions in the neighbouring river. They say that this custom has been kept up for many centuries. About two miles from these rivers is a cave with a narrow mouth but so spacious within and with so many ramifications that it is difficult to find one's way out again. They believe that the ashes of God are hidden here.

Pilgrims come to this place from all parts of India and after worshipping the idol, take away with them some grains of charred rice as proof of their visit. This rice they believe to have been kept here for many centuries."

Thomas Herbert was another celebrated author and traveller. Herbert was born in York around A.D. 1600 and commenced his higher studies at Jesus College, Oxford. But later, he shifted to Trinity College, Cambridge for a brief period. After he left university, he applied to his relative William Herbert, Earl of Pembroke, for going abroad as a traveller. The Earl sent him in 1626 for a journey to Africa and Asia, where he spent a major part in Persia and India.

After four years of travel he went back to his country in 1630. Thomas Herbert described Ayodhya in his published work, *Some Years' Travels into Diverse Parts of Asia and Afrique.* He got it reprinted after revision in A.D. 1638. In this book he mentioned the many monuments and also the monument which was most memorable to him was the "pretty old castle of Ramachand built by a Bannyan Pagod of that name", which he described as an antique monument built by Ramachandra 9,94,500 years ago. He also recorded the presence of Brahmins recording the names of pilgrims. These travel accounts enjoyed a great reputation at the time of their publication and have since been considered the best that appeared in England prior to the close of the seventeenth century. From Herbert's account of Ayodhya published in the year 1632 A.D. the following facts emerge. There were many antique monuments at Ayodhya in 1630 A.D.

Among those, the most memorable, according to Herbert, was "... old castle built by Ramachand (Ramachandra) which from time immemorial merchants used to visit to wash away their sins in the holy River Saryu. Such acts of virtue is recorded by sincere Brahmanas (Brahmins)."

Thomas Herbert further provides information on Rama's significance and influence on this country.

"Ducerat (Dashrath), who beget Rama, a king so famous for piety and high attempts, that to this day his name is exceedingly honoured, so that when they say Ram-Ram, it's as if they should say 'all good betide you'. That is, all good will fall on you. From addressing Ram-Ram it is expected that all good would fall on the caller and listener."

French traveller Jean de Thevenot also wrote a book based on his travels in India in the year 1666 A.D. The book was translated in English and published in London in the year 1687 A.D. (*The India They Saw*, vol. III).

In the book Thevenot also confirms this practice of mutual salute, i.e 'Ram-Ram'. The name of the book was *The Travels of Monsieur de Thevenot.* He wrote, "The Indians render him divine honours in their pagodas and elsewhere; and when they salute their friends they repeat his name, saying Ram-Ram. Their adoration consists in joining their hands, as if they prayed, letting them fall very low, and then lifting them up again gently to their mouth, and last of all, in raising them over their heads."

A Voyage to Surrat, in the Year 1689, written by J.O. Vington also describes a practice by the Hindus of incessantly chanting 'Ram-Ram ' by the Hindus during their funeral.

Another description came from Joseph Tieffenthaler's written accounts in the form of book, *Descriptio Indiae*, i.e. Description of India. The Austrian Jesuit priest, who stayed in Avadh (1766-71) had lived in India for more than two decades and he was well versed with both Persian and Sanskrit; so his accounts on the existence of a temple at the birthplace of Lord Rama and how it was converted into a mosque are considered to be one of the most authentic. Tieffenthaler visited Ayodhya (then known as Fyzabad) and travelled the whole of Avadh (known as Oudh during that era) during 1766-1771. His book on geography *The Modern Traveller* (Volume IV, English Version) was published in 1828 in which he has presented concrete evidence of the existence of a temple at the birthplace of Lord Rama.

"The modern town extends the considerable way along the banks of the *Goggrah*, adjoining the new city of *Fyzabad* which during the government of Shujah-ud-Dowlah, was the seat of the court." Its appearance in 1770 is thus described by Tieffenthaler: "*Avad* called *Adjudea* by the learned Hindoos, is city of the highest antiquity. Its houses are, for the most part, only of mud, covered with straws or tiles; many however are of brick. The principal street running from S to N, is about a league (miles) in length; and the breadth of the city is somewhat less. Its western part, as well as northern, is situated on a hill; the northeastern quarter rests upon eminences; but towards Bangla, it is level. This town has now but a scanty population, since the foundation of *Bangla* and *Fyzabad*; a new town where Governor has established his residence, and to which a great number of inhabitants of *Oude* have removed... On the southern bank of Deva (or *Goggrah*) are found various buildings erected by the *Gentoos* (Hindu) in memory of Rama, extending from east to west. The most remarkable place is that which is called *Sorgodoari,* that is to say, the heavenly temple because they say that Rama carried away from thence to heaven all the inhabitants of the city. The deserted town was repeopled and restored to its former condition by the famous king of *Oojein* (King Vikramaditya of Ujjain). There was a temple here on the high bank of river.

"But a place more particularly famous is that which is called *Sitha Rassoee, the table of Sitha* (Sieta), wife of Rama; situated on an eminence to the south of the city. The emperor demolished the fortress called *Ramcote*, and erected on the site a Mohammedan temple with a triple dome. According to others, it was erected by Babur. There are to be seen fourteen columns of black stone, five spans in height, which occupy the site of the fortress. Twelve of these columns now support the interior arcades of the mosque; the two others form part of the tomb of a certain Moor. They tell us, that these columns, or rather these remains of skilfully wrought columns, were brought from the Isle of Lanka or Selendip (Ceylon) by Hanuman, king of the monkeys.

"On the left is seen a square chest, raised five inches from the ground, covered with lime, about five *ells* in length by not more than four in breadth. The Hindoos call it *bedi*, the cradle; and the reason is, that there formerly stood here the house in which *Beshan* (Vishnu) was born in the form of Rama, and where also, they say, his three brothers were born. Afterwards, *Aurungzebe*, or, according to others, Babur caused the place to be destroyed, in order to deprive the heathen of the opportunity of practicing there their superstitions. Nevertheless, they still pay a superstitious reverence to both these places; namely, to that on which the natal dwelling of Rama stood, by going three times round it, prostrate on the earth. The two places are surrounded with a low wall adorned with battlements. Not far from this is a place where they dig up grains of black rice changed into little stones, which are affirmed to have been hidden underground ever since the time of Rama. On the 24th of the month *Tshet* (*Choitru*) a large concourse of people celebrate here the birthday of Rama, so famous throughout India. This vast city is only a mile distance from Bangla (Fyzabad) towards the E.N.E. On the high bank of river is a quadrangular fortress with low round towers. The walls are out of repair and it is unfurnished with inhabitants. Formerly, governors of the province resided here. Saadat Khan, frightened by an evil augury, transferred the government to Bangla. It is now completely destroyed."

With precision, Tieffenthaler mentioned the exact place

where Rama was born. In his accounts there is information regarding an existence of a natal house.

There was also mention of a place which was three to four miles from Fyzabad on Goggrah's southern bank. In his accounts, Tieffenthaler wrote:

"It is seated upon a hill somewhat steep, and fortified with little towers of earth at the four corners; in the middle is seen a subterrarranean hole, covered with a dome of moderate dimensions. Closeby is a lofty and very old tamarind tree. A piazza runs round it. It is said that Rama, after having vanquished the giant Ravana, and returned from Lanka, descended into this pit, and there disappeared: hence, they have given to this place the name of *Gouptar;* you have here then a descent into hell, as you had at Oude an ascension to heaven." As the scene of many of the leading events in the great epic poem of the *Ramayana*, *Oude* might be expected to abound with spots of traditional sanctity."

Tieffenthaler's accounts are generally considered to be both accurate and reliable. With such extensive details about Ayodhya and the then prevailing situation of the Ramjanmasthan, there is an impartiality. He made a clear mention about the demolition of Ramkot within which was situated the birthplace of Lord Rama. He also talked about a three-dome mosque that existed there. He was one of the first foreign travellers who had mentioned existence of Babri mosque in his book

A French scholar by the name of C. Mentelle also wrote about Ayodhya in great detail in his book, *Cosmography on Geography, on Chronology and on Ancient and Modern History.*

"*Avadh*, also known as *Aoude* and *Oude* in our country (France), and the learned Indian name it *Adjudea,* is one of the most ancient cities, situated on the banks of the River *Ghagra* and we consider that the tenth incarnation of Lord Vishnu happened in this city, in the form of Ramaji, whose father was the king of *Avadh*. The Indians come here from far off places on a big pilgrimage.

"In those days at Ayodhya there was an edifice called the celestial temple, from where it is said that Rama and Ramaji had taken to the heaven all the inhabitants of the city. This temple and several others were destroyed."

In A.D. 1783, William Hodges visited Ayodhya and made a beautiful sketch of Ayodhya on the saryu *ghat* (bank of Saryu river). In A.D. 1789 William Daniells visited Ayodhya and made certain sketches. He saw only Brahmins in the premises and interacted with them *(Ayodhya: Beyond Adduced Evidence by Kishore Kunal).*

Report by Montgomery Martin, British Surveryor (1838)

A local oral tradition of Ayodhya was first recorded in writing by Robert Montgomery Martin in 1838. It mentions that the city was deserted after the death of Rama's descendant, Brihadbala. It was King Vikramaditya of Ujjain who came searching for it. He not only cleared the forests that had covered the ancient ruins, but also re-established it and he got the Ramgarh Fort erected and built 360 temples.

Martin brought forward that the mosque was built on the ruins of Ramkot with pillars taken from Rama's palace, rather than of a building constructed by Vikramaditya, and the figures thereon having been damaged by the bigot (i.e. Babar) (Annexure 13, pp. 335-336 of Martin's: *History, Antiquities, Topography and Statistics of Eastern India*, vol. II).

In *East India Company Gazetteer of 1854* by Edward Thornton (a gazetteer is a documented geographical dictionary or directory containing particular descriptions of the empires, kingdoms, principalities, provinces, cities, towns, districts, fortresses, harbours, rivers, lakes, culture, customs, laws, etc.), there is a clear mention that Babur's mosque is embellished with 14 columns of elaborate workmanship taken from the old Hindu temple. It also mentions that the Hindus practised pilgrimage and devotion on the *Ramachabootra* (platform-like structure) which they believed to be Rama's cradle (Annexure 14, pp. 730-740 of Thornton's: *Gazetteer of the Territories under the Government of the East India Company*).

Surgeon General Edward Balfour was a Scottish surgeon, orientalist and pioneering environmentalist in India. He founded museums at Madras (currently known as Chennai) and Bangalore (Bengaluru); his ability with languages, particularly Hindi and later Persian helped him in getting transferred to a sepoy regiment. This led him to be posted to smaller areas and he spent the next ten years travelling around southern India. He was often sought by the English government as a translator of Hindustani and Persian. Balfour's collations on a variety of aspects of life in India led to the publication of *The Encyclopaedia of India and of Eastern and Southern Asia—Commercial, Industrial and Scientific,* first published in 1857 with subsequent editions titled as the *Encyclopaedia of India*. In *Encyclopaedia of India* (1858), there is mention of Ayodhya and the three mosques on the sites of three Hindu shrines: the *janmasthan*, the site where Rama was born; the *Swargadwar Mandir*, where his remains were buried; and the *Treta ka Thakur*, famed as the scene of one of his great sacrifices. (Annexure 15 from p. 56 of Balfour's *Encyclopaedia of India and of Eastern and Southern Asia)*.

Historical Sketch of Tehsil Fyzabad, a book written by P. Carnegy, who was the Officiating Commissioner and Settlement Officer of Faizabad, also gives details and precise description of the location of *Ramjanmasthan* and about Hindus worshipping at the place of birth of Rama amidst the conflict with Muslims.

He describes the Ramkot, palaces and *Ramjanmasthan* saying that the columns of *janmasthan* temple made of strong close-grained, dark, slate-coloured *kasauti* (or touch-stone) and carved with different devices were used by Muslims in the construction of Babur's mosque. He reports that until 1855, both Hindus and Muslims worshipped alike in the mosque-temple (see Annexure 16 for Carnegy's *Historical Sketch of Tehsil Fyzabad, Zilla Fyzabad, with the Old Capitals, Ajudhia and Fyzabad*, Lucknow 1970, pp. 5-7, 19-21 and a photograph taken by Carnegy). Another fact that came out of his report was that after proclamation of British rule in 1858, a great injustice was done to Hindus in the form of complete restrictions on them to worship inside the disputed structure. For the purpose, a railing was erected to keep the Hindus to worship on a platform outside the fence. All of these accounts of Carnegy have been further substantiated by the subsequent *gazetteers*.

Kishore Kunal gives an interesting account of Edward B. Eastwick, an Anglo-Indian, a relatively lesser known traveller in *Ayodhya Revisitied*. Eastwick was educated at Charterhouse and at Merton College, Oxford. He joined the Bombay infantry in 1836, but, owing to his talent for languages, was soon given a political post. In 1882 he wrote a book *Handbook of the Bengal Presidency*, which was published by John Murray, London. In this book Eastwick writes:

"The *janmasthan* or place where Ramachandra was born, is 1/3 of a.m. of the W. of the Hanumangarh. Close to the door and outside it, is a Muhammadan cemetery, in which 165 persons according to the *gazetteer*, are buried, all Muslims, who were killed in a fight between the Muslims and Hindus for the possession of the temple in 1855. The Muslims on that occasion charged up the steps of Hanumangarh, but were driven back with considerable loss. The Hindus followed up their success, and at the third attempt took the *janmasthan*, at the gates of which the Muslims who were killed were buried... Eleven Hindus were killed, and were thrown into the river."

Eastwick confirms that up to the advent of British rule in 1858, Hindus used to worship in the 'temple'. He writes:

"Since British rule, a railing has been put up, within which the Muslims pray. Outside the Hindus make their offerings. The actual *janmasthan* is a plain masonry platform, just outside the mosque or temple, but within the enclosure, on the left-hand side. The primeval temple perished, but was rebuilt by Vikram, and it was his temple that the Muslims converted into a mosque. Europeans are expected to take off their shoes if they enter the building, which is quite plain, with the exception of 12 black pillars taken from the old temple."

He further gives a detailed description of a pillar on the left of the door on which he saw some remains of a figure resembling Krishna or an *apsara*. Eastwick further provides substantive information about the steps of the pulpit which had an inscription which was illegible at the time he visited the temple. The inscription (containing Sanskrit hymns also had a picture of a Hindu deity) might have been of the demolished temple. The inscription which was different from the Persian inscription on the left and right of the pulpit, after prolonged and repeated trampling became unreadable.

"Eastwick also gave an important information about the Ramnavami fair in A.D 1880. Which was attended by five lakh devotees. And it was the time when the population was not very high," says Kishore Kunal.

Vishnu Bhatt Godse Versaikar left his native village Versai near Pune, on a journey to explore better earning options in the northern part of India in 1857. On 10 April, 1859 he managed to reach Ayodhya on the eve of Ramnavami festival. In his book *Majha Pravas* ('My Travels'), he gave a detailed description about the place and festivities. He narrated that around seven to eight lakh pilgrims from all over the country were in Ayodhya along with a large number of *sadhus* (ascetics). He wrote about the significance of bathing in Saryu river and paying homage to Lord Rama's birthplace on the auspicious day could wash away all sins. He wrote about devotees from other places speaking different languages and how in them he saw a strong bond of love and devotion for Rama, which tied them together. He further narrates:

"After the bath, the crowd left for the temple with *tulsi* leaves, areca nuts and coins clutched in their hands as offerings. Offering *tulsi* leaves to the Lord at this spot is said to be essentially beneficial. I too arrived, like others, with my offerings at the birthspot of Lord Rama. The fabled spot is merely a large, waist-height platform in an open area. It is made of limestone and surrounded by a wall about three or four feet high; grasses and weeds grow all over, and in the distance one can be seen the remains of what must have been the walls of an old fort. The place where Lord Rama's mother Kaushalya's palace is said to have stood is just a flat piece of land now. Several thousand excited pilgrims in an open space such as this can cause stampedes, so one has to be on one's guard all through. The administration also posts special pickets on this occasion to ward off unpleasant happenings and despite that, each year, five or six pilgrims lose their lives in the melee. Anyway, we finally viewed the sacred spot and came back."

He also describes stories related to *swargadwar* (gate to heaven) and Ayodhya. He visited Varanasi and other important places like Gwalior, Kanpur, Lucknow, Jhansi, Kalpi and Bundelkhand before returning back to his native place.

Some other *Gazetteers*

***Gazetteer of the Province Oudh* (1877)**: It stated that the Moghuls destroyed three important Hindu temples at Ayodhya and constructed mosques thereon. Babur built the Babri mosque on Ramjanmabhoomi in 1528, Aurangzeb built one on *swargadwar*, and either Aurangzeb or Shah Jahan did the same on *Treta-ka-Thakur*. All other assertions from Carnegy's *Historical Sketch of Faizabad* are confirmed in this *gazetteer* (Annexure 17: *Gazetteer of the Province of Oudh*, vol. I, 1877, pp. 6-7).

***Imperial Gazetteer of Faizabad* (1881):** It confirms the construction of three Moghul mosques at Ayodhya on the site of three celebrated shrines, viz. *janmasthan, swargadwar* and *Treta-ka-Thakur* (Annexure 18: *Imperial Gazetteer of India, Provincial Series, United Provinces of Agra and Oudh*, vol. II, pp. 338-9).

***Barabanki District Gazetteer* by H.R. Neville (1902):** Neville reports that "numerous disputes have sprung up from time to time between the Hindu priests and the Mussalmans of Ayodhya with regard to the ground on which formerly stood the *janmasthan* temple, which was destroyed by Babur and replaced by a mosque" (Annexure 21: Neville: *Barabanki District Gazetteer*, Lucknow 1902, p. 168-169).

***Faizabad District Gazetteer* by H.R. Neville (1905):** This chronicle confirms that the *janmasthan* temple marking the birthplace of Rama at Ramkot was destroyed by Babur and replaced by a mosque using the materials and columns of the temple. In spite of its desecration, Hindus continued to regard it as a holy spot. The desecration caused numerous disputes and clashes between the communities (*see* Annexure 22, Neville: *Fyzabad District Gazetteer*, Lucknow 1905, pp. 172-177).

***Court Verdict* by Col. F.E.A. Chamier, District Judge, Faizabad (1886):** In delivering his judgement in Civil Appeal No. 27 of 1885, the judge, after visiting the Babri mosque site for personal inspection, observed :"It is most unfortunate that a *masjid* should have been built on land specially held sacred by the Hindus, but as that event occurred 356 years ago, it is too late now to remedy the grievance" (Annexure 19: extract reproduced from *Muslim India*, March 1986, p. 107).

***Archaeological Survey of India Report* by A. Fuhrer**

(1891): Fuhrer accepts that Mir Khan built the Babri mosque on the site of the Ramjanmabhoomi temple, using many of its columns. He also confirmed that Aurangzeb had constructed two other mosques in Ayodhya on the sites of *swargadwar* and *Treta-ka-Thakur* temples (Annexure 20, Fuhrer: *The Monumental Antiquities and Inscriptions in the North-west Provinces and Oudh*, ASI Report, 1891, pp. 296-297).

Archaeological Survey of India (1934): It identified all the holy sites of Ayodhya with reference to the ancient texts, numbered them and put up sign posts in stone to mark the sites. The Babri mosque was identified as the Ramjanmabhoomi and a sign post was embedded there saying: 'Site no. 1: Janmabhoomi.'

***Baburnama in English* by Annette Beveridge (1920):** After analysing the inscriptions on the Babri mosque and studying the archaeological features, she says that Babur was impressed with the dignity and sanctity of the ancient Hindu shrine it displaced, and that as an obedient follower of Muhammad, Babur regarded the substitution of the temple by a mosque as dutiful and worthy. (Annexure 23, Beveridge: *Baburnama* in English, vol. II., 1922, appendix on the inscriptions on Babur's Mosque in Ajodhya (Oudh), p. xxvii-xxix).

***Encyclopaedia Britannica* (1978, 15th edition, vol. I)**: This most authentic encyclopaedia records that Rama's birthplace is marked by a mosque erected by the Moghul emperor Babur in 1528 on the site of an earlier temple. The encyclopaedia also provides a photograph of the present structure, describing it as the mosque on Rama's birthplace, Ayodhya, U.P., India. Earlier editions of the encyclopaedia also contained this information (Annexure 25 : E.B., vol. I, p. 693).

***Ayodhya* by Hans Bakker (1984)**: In his most comprehensive study, the Dutch scholar Bakker has repeatedly and categorically accepted that an old Vaishnava temple was situated on the holy spot where Rama descended on earth. It was destroyed by Babur in 1528 and a mosque was built on it. The black-stone pillars of the temple were utilised by Mir Baqi in the construction. Two more pillars have been driven upside down into the ground at the grave of the Muslim Sufi saint, Musa Ashiqan, who is said to have incited Babur to demolish the *janmabhoomi* temple. Bakker concludes that Ramjanmabhoomi temple was one of the oldest Rama temples in the country to be in existence in the 12th century. (cfr. Bakker: *Ayodhya*, Egbert Forsten, Groningen 1986, part I, pp. 43-59, 60-66, 119-153, part II, pp. 118-121, 143-149, 173-175).

□

3

Demolishing Temple, Building Mosque

Since A.D. 712 , Muslim invaders attacked Bharat followed by demolition of temples and construction of mosques and *madrasas.*

Mohammad Bin Qasim invaded Sindh in A.D. 712 After defeating King Dahir of Sindh, he demolished various Hindu institutions and converted a large number of Hindus forcefully into Islam.

In A.D. 1000, Mahmud Gaznavi attacked Bharat and defeated Raja Jaipal. In A.D. 1008 he won Kangra and in A.D. 1011 he won Thaneshwar where he demolished a number of Hindu temples, including Chakraswami temple. In A.D. 1025, he demolished Somnath temple and broke the main idol into several pieces.

Sita Ram Goel has listed in detail the destruction of Hindu temples in his pioneering work *Hindu Temples: What Happened to Them* (Vols. I and II). Summing up the macabre destruction, Goel says (*Hindu Temples: What Happened to Them,* pp. 246, Vols. II).

"The temples were attacked 'all along the way' as the armies of Islam advanced; they were robbed of their scriptural wealth, pulled down, laid waste, burnt with naptha, trodden under horse's hoofs and destroyed from their very foundations till not a trace of them remained. Mahmud of Ghazni robbed and burnt down 1,000 temples at Mathura and

10,000 temples in and around Kannauj. One of his successors, Ibrahim demolished 1,000 temples each in Ganga-Yamuna *doab* and Malwa. Muhammad Gori destroyed another 1,000 at Varanasi. Qutubud'din Aibak employed elephants for pulling down 1,000 temples in Delhi. Ali Adil Shah of Bijapur destroyed 200 to 300 temples in Karnataka. A Sufi, Qayim Shah, destroyed 12 temples at Tiruchirapalli. Such exact or approximate counts, however, are available only in a few cases. Most of the time we are informed that "many strong temples which would have remained unshaken even by the trumpets blown on the day of judgement, were levelled to the ground when swept by Islam."

The above details have been made available by the Muslim historians themselves. Goel pointed out in his seminal work (pp. 246), "We find the Muslim historians going into raptures as they describe the scenes of desecration and destruction. For Amir Khusro it was an occasion to show the power of his poetic imagination. When Jalaludin Khilji wrought havoc at Jhain, 'A cry rose from the temples as if a second Mahmud had taken birth.' The temples in the environs of Delhi were 'bent in prayers' and 'made to do prostration', by Alauddin Khilji. When the temple of Somnath was destroyed and its debris thrown into the sea towards the west, the poet rose to his full height. "So the temple of Somnath", he wrote, "was made to bow towards the holy Mecca, and the temple lowered its head and jumped into the sea, so you may say that the building first said its prayers and then had a bath."

Many historians including the Muslims have similarly captured the demolition of the Rama temple in Ayodhya in A.D. 1528 by Babur. It was done to build a mosque there. A section of historians have argued that this didn't happen during Babur's regime but this happened during Aurangzeb's regime. However, as one looks at the historical evidence, one comes to know how the Rama temple was demolished at Ayodhya and a mosque was built there.

One of the most credible evidences regarding this has come from the land revenue records. The first *Report of Settlement of the Land Revenue of Fyzabad District* by K.F. Mitchell (vide paragraphs 618-19 and 666-669) traces the past history of '*janmasthan*/Babri Masjid' in 'Kot Ramachandra/ Ayodhya'. It confirms the fact that Babur came to Ayodhya in 1528 and halted there for a week, during which he destroyed the *janmasthan* temple and on its site built a mosque, using largely the materials of the old structure. The author of this report further adds that according to Scyder's memoirs of Babur, the latter encamped about 5 or 6 miles from Ayodhya and stayed for a week.

There were two inscriptions inside the mosque which were damaged during the riots in 1934 and were later restored. The one which was originally there on the southern side of the pulpit reads as under:

'By order of King Babur whose justice is an edifice, meeting the place of the sky, this descending place of angels was built by the fortune-favoured noble Mir Baqi. The good will remain everlasting and when I utter the words, 'the goodwill remain everlasting', the year of its erection becomes manifest.'

Now for the expression, 'the good will remain everlasting', the Persian original is *buwad khair baqi* which rendered into cardinal numbers comes to 935 A.H./1528 A.D., as under:

b = 2
w = 6
d = 4
kh = 600
i = 10
r = 200
b = 2
a = 1

q = 100
i = 10
Total = 935

Some historians have erred in dating the event as 923 or 930 A.H. instead of 935 A.H. due to misreading of the date given above in the form of Arabic/Persian alphabets arranged into words which are : 'b u w a d k h a i r b a q i'. What they have done is that they dropped 'b u w a d'.

There are several Muslim sources which shed light on the existence and demolition of the Ramjanmabhoomi.

Allamah Muhammad Najmu mentions (*I-Ghani Khan Rampuri, Tarikh-I-Avadh*, vol. V, pp. 200-201), "At Ajodhya, where there stood the temple of Ramachandraji's *janmsthan*, there is *Sitaji-ki-Rasoi*, adjacent to it, King Babur got a magnificent mosque built there, which is the Jami Masjid, in 933 A.H. under the patronage of Sayyid Musa' Ashiqan, the date of which is Khayr Baqi (923). Till date the mosque is called Masjid-i-Sita-ki-Rasoi and that temple is extant by the side... Babur got the mosque built after demolishing the *janmasthan*, and used in his mosque the stone of the same *Janmasthan*, which was richly engraved, had precious kasauti stone and which survives even today."

Muraqqahi-Khusrawi, otherwise known as *Tawarikh-i-Avadh*, by Shykh 'Azamat' Ali Kakorawi Nami (1811-93) who happened to be an eye-witness to much that happened during Wajid Ali Shah's regime, was completed in 1869 but was published only in 1986. Later it was published again under the title, *Amir Ali Shahid aur Ma'rakah-i-Hanumangadhi*. Its opening paragraph says, "According to old records, it has been a religious rule with Muslim rulers, after the triumph of Sayyid Salar Mas'ud Ghazi to build mosques, monasteries and inns, spread Islam and put a stop to blasphemous practices (*bid'at*), wherever they found manifestation of infidelity. Accordingly, even as they cleared up Mathura, Brindaban, etc. from the rubbish of non-Islamic practices, the magnificent Babri mosque (*Masjid-i-sarbaland-i-Bahari*) came up in 923 A.H."

Fasanah-i-Ibrat, written by Mirza Raja All Beg Surur (1787-1867) in 1860 *circa* but published first in 1884, says that a glorious sky-high mosque was built during Babur's regime on the spot where Sita-ki-Rasoi is situated in Avadh.

There are several texts which clearly mention that a Muslim *faqir* by the name of Sayyid Mir Musa Ashiqan also played an important role in the demolition of the temple at Ramjanmabhoomi and its replacement by a mosque-like structure.

A work in Persian written by a Muslim *faqir*, *Mawalayiyy Abu-i-Karim*, who belonged to the line of Musa Ashiqan, was later translated into Urdu and published in 1979. Another edition of this book titled, *Gumashta Hatat-i-Ajodhya* Ya'ni *Tarikh-Parinahi-Madinatu* was published in 1981. Interestingly, while the earlier edition gave details of how at the behest of Musa Ashiqan the Rama temple was demolished by Babur, these details went missing in the 1981 edition!

Quoting from some of the original works in Persian, Lala Sita Ram says in *Ayodhya ka Itihaasa* (pp.150), "... how Babur was led to destroy the Rama temple and erect the existing structure on its site is that he visited Musa Ashiqan during his stay at Ayodhya in 1528 itself. The *faqir* asked him to demolish the temple and erect a mosque on its site. Babur was hesitant at first but succumbed to the *faqir's* wishes..."

□

4
Muslim Scholars on Ramjanmabhoomi

It is an established fact now that Babur had destroyed the temple at the birthplace of Lord Rama in 1528 and built a mosque-like structure there.

John Leyden translated the memoirs of Babur in 1819. William Erkshire is known to have found a document in 1826 confirming Babur's stay in Ayodhya. In 1922, Annet S. Beveridge translated memoirs of Babur in English again. All of them confirm that Babur encamped in Ayodhya in 1828.

Though many European travellers and historians have provided clinching evidence including notes in several official documents of the British rule in India, that the temple at Lord Rama's birthplace was replaced by a mosque, those who disagree with this argument often allege that the pro-temple camp quotes British sources which were biased against Muslims.

However, there are enough Muslim sources also which clearly show that the temple at Lord Rama's birthplace was destroyed. Noted historian Harsha Narain (*Indian Express*, 26 February, 1990 and *Hindu Temples: What Happened to Them*, vol. I, pp. 169 to 175 (ed.), Sitaram Goel, Voice of India publications) has cited "certain purely Muslim resources beyond the sphere of British influence to show that the Babri mosque has displaced a Hindu temple—the Ramjanmasthan temple, to be precise—wholly or partly."

Here is what Narain has to say: "First, an indirect evidence. In an application dated November 30, 1858 filed by one Muhammad Asghar, Khatib and Muezzin, Babri Masjid, to initiate legal proceedings against, 'Bairagiyan-i-Janmasthan'. The Babri Masjid has been called '*Masjid-i-janmasthan* and the courtyard near the arch and the pulpit within the boundary of the mosque, *maqam janmasthan ka*. The Bairagis had raised a platform in the courtyard which the applicant wanted to be dismantled. He has mentioned that the place of *janmasthan* had been lying unkempt/in disorder (*parishan)* for hundreds of years and that the Hindus performed worship there."

Narain says, "... the Hindus had all along been carrying out their worship, all that implies that there must have been some construction there as a part of (*janmasthan*) temple, which Mir Baqi partly demolished and partly converted into the existing Babri mosque... And the Hindus had no alternative but to make *do* with the temple-less courtyard. Otherwise, it is simply unthinkable that they might have been performing worship for such a long time and on such a sacred place without a proper temple."

Narain futher quotes *Hadiqah-i-Shubada* as another Muslim source to prove how temples including the one on the birthplace of Lord Rama were destroyed by Mughals. Mirza Jaan, the author of *Hadiqah-i-Shubada* was an active participant in the *jihad* led by Amir Aki Amethawi during Wajid Ali Shah's regime in 1855 for recapture of Hanumangarhi (a few hundred yards from the Babri mosque) from the Hindus, says Narain. He further adds, "The book was ready just after the failure of the *jihad* and saw the light of day in the following year, viz. in 1856, at Lucknow. Rai's Ahmad Jafari, has included it as Chapter IX in his book entitled *Wajid Ali Shah aur Unka Ahd* (Lucknow: Kitab Manzil, 1957) after however, omitting what he considered unnecessary, but without adding a word from his side."

Mirza Jaan states, "Wherever they found magnificent temples of the Hindus ever since the establishment of Syed Salar Mas'ud Ghazi's rule, the Muslim rulers in India built mosques, monasteries and inns, appointed muezzins, teachers and store-stewards, spread Islam vigorously, and vanquished the *kafirs*. Likewise, they cleared up Faizabad and Avadh, too, from the filth of reprobation (infidelity) because it was a great centre of worship and capital of Rama's father. Where there stood the great temple (of *Ramjanmasthan*), there they built a big mosque, and where there was a small *mandap* (pavilion), there they erected a camp mosque *(masjid-i-mukhtasar-i-qanati)*. The *janmasthan* temple is the principle place of Rama's incarnation, adjacent to which is the *Sita-ki-Rasoi*. Hence, what a lofty mosque was built there by King Babur in 923 A.H. (A.D. 1528), under the patronage of Musa Ashiqan! The mosque is still known far and wide as the *Sita-ki-Rasoi* mosque. And that temple is extant by its side."

According to Narain, "It must be borne in mind that Mirza Jaan claims to write all this on the basis of older records (*Kutub-i-Sabiqah*) and contemporary accounts.

Another Muslim source quoted by Narain is a chapter of the *Muraqqah-i Khusrawi*. This text is also known as *Tarikh-i Avadh*. It was written by Azamat Ali Kakorawi Nami (1811-1893). He was known to be an eyewitness to what happened during the regime of Wajid Ali Shah.

Narain reveals how the facts from this book regarding Ayodhya were repressed deliberately to manipulate the historical facts. Nami had completed this work in 1869, but (it) could not see the light of the day for over a century. One manuscript of it is extant and that is in the Tagore Library of Lucknow University. A press copy of it was prepared by Dr. Zaki Kakorawi for publication with the financial assistance of the Fakkhruddin Ali Ahmad Memorial Committee, Uttar Pradesh, Lucknow.

The committee vetoed the publication of its chapter dealing with the *jihad* led by Amir Ali Amethawi for recapture of Hanumangarhi from the Bairagis, from its funds, on the ground that its publication would not be opportune in view of the prevailing political situation, with the result that Dr. Kakorawi had to publish the book minus that chapter in 1986, for the first time. Later, however, he published the chapter separately and independently of any financial or other assistance from the committee in 1987 from the Markaz-i-Adab-i-Urdu, 137, Shahganj, Luncknow-3 under the title *Amir, Ali Shahid aur Ma'rkah-i-Hanumangarhi.*

There are great similarities in Shykh Nami's *Tarikh-i Avadh* and what Mirza Jaan wrote. Nami says in the beginning of his work, "According to old records, it has been a rule with the Muslim rulers from the first to build mosques, monasteries and inns, spread Islam, and put (a stop to) non-Islamic practices, wherever they found prominence (of *kufr*). Accordingly even as they cleared up Mathura, Bindraban, etc. from the rubbish of non-Islamic practices, the Babri mosque was built up in 923 A.H. under the patronage of Sayyid Musa Ashiqan in the *janmasthan* temple *(butkhane janmasthan mein)* in Faizabad-Avadh, which was a great place of (worship) and capital of Rama's father.

Another important Muslim source is a text titled *Fasnah-i-Ibrat* by well-known early Urdu novelist, Mirza Rajab Ali Beg Surur (1787-1867). An excerpt from this was appended to Dr. Kakorawin in Nami's book. According to this excerpt, as quoted by Narain, a great mosque was built on the spot where 'Sita-ki-Rasoi is situated. During the regime of Babur, the Hindus had no guts to be a match for Muslims. The mosque was built in 923 A.H. (A.D. 1528) under the patronage of Sayyid Mir Ashiqan. Aurangzeb built a mosque on the Hanumangarhi. ...The Bairagis effaced the mosque and erected a temple in its place. Then idols began to be worshipped openly in the Babri mosque where the *Sita-ki-Rasoi* is situated."

Historian Meenakshi Jain (*Ram & Ayodhya,* Aryan Books International, pp. 121-123) has brought out some more interesting Muslim sources in this context. "In 1822, an official of the Faizabad law court, Hafizullah, also stated that the 'mosque founded by Babur is situated at the birthplace of Rama" (Noorani, *Frontline,* 17.7.1998).

Subsequent testimony of Hindu devotion to Ayodhya came from an unlikely source. On 12th August, 1855, Wajid Ali Shah (1847-56), the last Nawab of Avadh, sent a *purcha* (note) to British resident, Major James Outram, to which were attached five documents confirming the long drawn out contest between Hindus and Muslims (N.A.I., Foreign Department Political, 28 December 1855, No. 351-358&KW). The documents were:

1. A document from Muhammad Nihalal-ud-din, the *darogah* of Avadh, deputed by the king to ascertain whether any *masjid* exists in Hanumangarhi.
2. A document from Hafeezullah, *darogah* of Fyzabad.
3. A document from the Imam of Fyzabad.
4. A copy of a paper sealed with the seal of the Qazi of Fyzabad, dated A.D. 1735.
5. A sealed statement by forty of the principal inhabitants of Fyzabad on the disturbances between Hindus and Muslims.

The *purcha* stated a similar quarrel over the *masjid* built "by one of the former sovereigns of Delhi that this fact is notorious" had arisen in the time of Burhan-ul-Mulk-Saadat Khan (1722-1739), the first Nawab of Avadh. But the Hindus had afterwards declared that they had no intention of "meddling with the mosque".

The Nawab asserted that "the tenor of all these papers cast (sic) all the blame on the Hindoos and details their atrocities." He further asserted, "A fence which was erected in the present king's reign to separate *masjid* from the Hindu place of worship has been torn down." On the day of the burial of the Mahommedans, who were put into one pit near the door of the *masjid*, "the Hindus sacrificed a pig in the *masjid* and blew their shells." They also destroyed the tomb of martyr Khawjah Hutee, which was near the *Masjid*. The Nawab complained that the Bairagis were not very large in numbers but were 'largely assisted' by the followers of Raja Man Singh and Raja Kishan Dutt and other *zamindars*. A large number of families had abandoned Avadh and retired to Fyzabad.

The British Resident in his reply dated 14th August 1855, commented that the enclosed representations were "obviously untrue in one particular" inasmuch as they laid the entire blame on the Hindus (N.A.I. Foreign Department Political, 28 December 1855; 351-8&KW).

□

5

1949: The Turning Point

Ayodhya and particularly the Ramjanmabhoomi has witnessed continuous struggle to reclaim the birthplace of Lord Rama since the demolition of the temple in 1528.

Despite demolition of the temple and construction of a mosque by Babur, the devotees of Lord Rama continued to worship at Ramjanmabhoomi.

Tristhalisetu (literature on how to conduct religious ceremonies at holy places by Pandit Narayana Bhatta, one of the most authentic texts on Hinduism) specified three situations in which worshipping should be continued (*Ayodhya: Beyond Adduced Evidence* by Kishore Kunal). These three situations are:

1. If an idol has been taken off from the original place and no other idol has substituted it, then whatever remains there should be worshipped as the place has the same sanctity as that of an idol.
2. If an idol has been substituted by another idol, the new idol should be worshipped.
3. If there is a situation when there would be no idol, such as the one during Muslim rule, then the spot shall be worshipped. The site gets the status of a deity. Hence when the *janmabhoomi* temple was destroyed at Ayodhya by Babur, the devotees started worshipping the *bedi* (cradle).

The case for Ramjanmabhoomi took an important turn within two years of India attaining independence. In 1949 an application was submitted to the UP government by the devotees of Lord Rama seeking permission to construct a temple at the *Ramjanmasthan* (birthplace of Lord Rama). In a letter dated 20 July, 1949, the then Deputy Secretary of the UP government sought response of Faizabad's District Magistrate K.K.K. Nayar in this letter. A copy was also sent to Commissioner, Faizabad division.

The District Magistrate submitted his report on 10 October, 1949. The report said, "Hindu public has put in this application with a view to erect a decent and *vishal* (big) temple in place of the small one which exists at present. There is nothing in the way and permission can be given as Hindu population is very keen to have a nice temple at the place where Bhagwan Ramachandraji was born. The land where temple is to be erected is of *nazul*."

Nayar wrote an interesting letter to the Home Secretary, UP government on 16 December, 1949. The letter was written in response to a wireless message he had received around a week earlier from the Home Secretary.

Nayar attached the site plan as an annexure with this letter, showing the position of Babri Masjid and Lord Rama's temple at Ramjanmabhoomi. He also stated in this letter that a magnificent temple at the site was constructed by Vikramaditya in 16th century. It was not only demolished by Babur but the mosque known as Babri Masjid was constructed on it and in the said process, building material of the temple was used. He further added that it was a long time before Hindus were again restored the possession of a site therein, i.e. at the corner of two walls. It is further mentioned that "Muslims who go to the mosque pass in front of the temple and there has frequently been trouble over the occasional failure of Muslims to take off their shoes."

Here are some excerpts from the reports submitted by the district administration of Faizabad to the Home Department of UP government in December, 1949:

"Sometime this year, probably in October or November, some grave-mounds were partially destroyed apparently by Bairagis who very keenly resent Muslim association with this shrine. On 12.11.49 a police picket was posted at this place. The picket still continues in augmented strength.

"There were since other attempts to destroy grave-mounds. Four persons were caught and cases are proceeding against them but for quite some time now there have been no attempts. Muslims, mostly of Faizabad, have been exaggerating these happenings and giving currency to the report that graves are being demolished systematically on a large scale. This is an entirely false canard inspired apparently by a desire to prevent Hindus from securing in this area possession or rights of a larger character than they have been enjoying so far."

Even as the officials were exchanging correspondence at various levels on the issue of Rama temple, the Hindus claimed on the night of 22-23 December, 1949 that Ram Lalla (Lord Rama in the child form) had revealed himself. This revelation was claimed to be in the form of an idol in the *garbha griha* (sanctum sanctorum). However, those who were opposed to the Rama temple, claimed that the idol was kept deliberately by some ascetics of Ayodhya.

On 23 December, 1949, an FIR was filed by Sub-Inspector Ram Deo Dubey, the incharge of local police station in this case.

Earlier in a letter dated 29 November, 1949, the Faizabad SP, Kripal Singh, had expressed grave apprehension regarding entry of Hindus in the mosque for allegedly installing a deity on 30 November, 1949.

But Kripal Singh informed his superiors in a letter dated 2 February, 1950 that the incident of 23.12.1949 could not have been predicted. The District Magistrate Nayar wrote in his report/diary, it is mentioned, that on 23.12.1949 the crowd was controlled by permitting some select persons to perform certain rituals, i.e. Abhiram Dass, Ram Shukal Dass and Sudarshan Dass.

It was also mentioned in this report that the removal of the idol as desired by the state government was not possible and it would lead to slaughter and would be most inadvisable. In the entry of 25.12.1949, it is mentioned that rituals of *puja* and *bhog* were performed as usual. The entry in the diary/ report at 9.30 a.m. dated 27 December, 1949 says that the D.M. outrightly refused to abide by the direction of the government to remove the idol "and that if government still insisted that removal should be carried out in the face of these facts, I would request to replace me by another officer."

The DM, Faizabad wrote two letters, dated 26 and 27 December, 1949 to Bhagwan Sahai, Chief Secretary, government of UP. In these letters also he insisted that the incident that happened on the midnight of 22-23 December, 1949 was unpredictable and irreversible. He rather castigated the government for showing so much interest.

In the letter dated 26 December, 1949 and addressed to Chief Secretary Bhagwan Sahai, Nayar not only expressed his inability to the possibility of removing the idol, but clearly mentioned, "the immense public sympathy in support of this cause." He stated, "The mosque can be entered only through the temple premises and is so accessible at all times. Further, the temple premises are occupied at all hours and the mosque is deserted all the time except for one hour during Friday prayer. To prevent determined Hindus from getting into the mosque, either by force or in secret, the mosque had to be permanently policed."

Nayar also mentioned about the huge cost of the policing "a deserted and almost unused mosque permanently."

It is also of great significance that no Muslim came forward to lodge an FIR or complain of dispossession or obstruction in his alleged use of the *masjid*.

In another letter to Chief Secretary, Nayar wrote about being informed to carry out a scheme of removing the idol from the mosque. This, according to him, would prove to be a great threat to the peace between communities in the entire district. According to him, "The depth of feelings behind the movement and the desperate nature of the resolves and vows in support of it should not be underestimated."

He further added, "I shall also be unable to find in the district a Hindu, let alone a qualified priest, who will be prepared on any inducement to undertake the removal of the idol."

In the report/diary dated 30.12.1949 it is mentioned that when Chief Secretary visited the spot, he was surrounded by the crowd which uttered loud cries of, "*Bhagwan ka phatak khol do*, (Open the doors of the Lord)."

On 29 December, 1949, preliminary order under Section 145, Cr.P.C. was issued by Markandey Singh, Additional City Magistrate, Faizabad-cum-Ayodhya and simultaneously attachment order was also passed treating the situation to be of emergency. The disputed site was directed to be given in the receivership of Priya Datt Ram, Chairman, Municipal Board. The complete order is quoted below:

"Whereas I, Markandey Singh, Magistrate First Class and Additional City Magistrate, Faizabad-cum-Ayodhya, I am fully satisfied from information received from police sources and from other credible sources that a dispute between Hindus and Muslims in Ayodhya over the question of rights of proprietorship and worship in the building claimed variously as Babri Masjid and *Janmabhoomi Mandir*, situated at *Mohalla* Ramkot within the local limits of my jurisdiction, is only to lead to a breach of the peace. I hereby direct the parties described below namely: 1) Muslims who are bonafide residents of Ayodhya or who claim rights of proprietorship or worship in the property in dispute; 2) Hindus who are bonafide residents of Ayodhya or who claim rights of proprietorship or worship in the property in dispute, to appear before me on 17th day of January at 11 a.m. at Ayodhya Police Station in person or by pleader and put in written statements of their respective claims with regard to the fact of actual possession of the subject of dispute. And the case being one of emergency, I hereby attach the said buildings pending decision.

"The attachment shall be carried out immediately by Station Officer, Ayodhya Police Station, who shall then put the attached properties in the charge of Sri Priya Datt Ram, Chairman, Municipal Board, Faizabad-cum-Ayodhya, who shall thereafter be the receiver thereof and shall arrange for the care of the property in dispute. The receiver shall submit for approval a scheme for management of the property in dispute during attachment and the cost of management shall be defrayed by the parties to this dispute in such proportions as may be fixed from time to time. This order shall, in the absence of information regarding the actual names and addresses of the 38 parties to the dispute to be served by publication in: 1. The English daily, *The Leader*, Allahabad, 2. The Urdu weekly, *Akhtar*, Faizabad, 3. The Hindi weekly *Virakta Ayodhya*. Copies of this order shall also be affixed to the walls of the buildings in dispute and to the notice-board at Ayodhya Police Station. Given under my hand and the seal of the court on this the twenty ninth day of December, 1949 at Ayodhya."

At the end of the para beginning with 'the attachment' there was a line which was admittedly scored off by the Magistrate himself. The Magistrate admitted it in his reply/ response to the Transfer Application filed in this court for transfer of the case under Section 145, Cr.P.C. The Magistrate stated that he scored off the sentence before signing the order as it was redundant. The original records of proceedings under Section 145, Cr.P.C. have been summoned in these suits. The cutting does not bear initials. The sentence is readable with great difficulty. It is to the effect that *puja/darshan* shall continue as was being done at that time (presently). Sri Priya Datt Ram took charge on 05.01.1950 and made an inventory of the attached properties. Items No.1 to 14 and 16 to 20 were related to movable properties, including idols. Item No.15 was related to the building which states the same to be three-domed building along with courtyard and boundary wall and eastern boundary is shown as *chabootara mandir* of Rama under the ownership of *nirmohi akhara* and courtyard of the same *mandir*. Towards north the boundary mentioned is *hata chhatti* courtyard and *nirmohi akhara*. The receiver Sri Priya Datt Ram submitted the scheme of management to the DM (in accordance with preliminary order) stating that "the most important item of management is the maintenance of *bhog* and *puja* in the condition in which it was carried on when I took over charge."

Muslims admit that since 23.12.1949, they have not been able to offer the prayers in the mosque.

According to the Muslims and some Hindu parties in the suits, the idol of Lord Rama which was on the *chabootara* in the outer courtyard, was placed/transferred under the central dome of the building. According to the further case of the Muslims, the idol was placed on *mimbar* (pulpit) in the *meharab* (arch) under central dome from where on Fridays, the Imam (who leads the congregation prayers) used to read *khutba* (sermon, before Friday prayer).

It appears that since 23.12.1949, firstly under the directions of the executive authorities and thereafter, under the order of the Magistrate passed in proceedings under Section 145, Cr.P.C., only two or three Pandits were permitted to go inside the place where the idol was kept to perform religious ceremonies like *bhog* and *puja,* etc. and general public was permitted to have *darshan* only from beyond the grill-brick wall. These 41 suits, popularly known as title suits, were instituted before Civil Judge, Faizabad on 16.01.1950, 17.12.1959, 18.12.961 and 01.07.1989 respectively.

The information about the developments happening in Ayodhya also reached the national capital with Deputy Prime Minister Sardar Vallabhbhai Patel writing a letter to Chief Minister of UP, Govind Ballabh Pant (9 January, 1950), expressing his view that the issue should be resolved amicably in a spirit of mutual tolerance and goodwill between the two communities. He wrote, "I realise there is a great deal of sentiment behind the move which has taken place. At the same time, such matters can only be resolved peacefully if we take the willing consent of the Muslim community with us."

However, more than the sentiments of the vast majority of Hindus, the then Prime Minister Jawaharlal Nehru was more concerned about the impact of these developments on minorities as well as Kashmir.

On 16 January, 1950, Gopal Visharad filed a suit (Regular Suit No.2 of 1950, hereinafter referred to as Suit No.1). Visharad, the plaintiff, claimed in the plaint that he was worshipping the *janmabhoomi*, idol of Bhagwan Sri RamachandraJi and *charan paduka* (foot impression). The boundaries indicated that in the East there was *bhandar* and *chabootara*, in the north Sita-ki-Rasoi and *parti* towards west and south. It presumably related to the constructed portion and the inner courtyard. It was further pleaded that for several days, due to illness, plaintiff was not going to the disputed place, building/ site for worship and on 14.01.1950, when he went there for worship and *darshan*, defendant No. 6, i.e. state of U.P., Lucknow and its employees prevented the petitioner from going inside where idols of Shri Ramachandra and others were placed and that it was done on the undue insistence of defendants 1 to 5 (all Muslim residents of Ayodhya, who all have now died and have not been substituted). It was also mentioned in the plaint that the state and its employees, i.e. respondents No.7 to 9, K.K.K. Nayar, Deputy Commissioner, Faizabad, Markandey Singh, Additional City Magistrate, Faizabad and Ram Kripal Singh, S.P., Faizabad (whose names have now been deleted and only the designations remain) were unduly pressurising the Hindu public for removal of the idols from the existing place. The relief claimed was that it be declared that the plaintiff according to his religion and custom is entitled to do worship and *darshan* of Sri Bhagwan Ramachandra and others at the place of *janmabhoomi* by going near the idols without any let or hindrance and defendants No. 6 & 9 have no right to interfere in the said rights. Prohibitory injunction was also sought against defendants No. 6 to 10 (defendant No.10 is Sunni Central Waqf Board of U.P., added in 1989). Defendant No.11 is Nirmohi Akhara, added in 1990. The injunction sought was that defendants No.6 to 10 should not remove the idols of Bhagwan Ramachandra and others from the place where the idols were and they should also not close the way leading to that and should not interfere in worship and *darshan* in any manner. The original plaintiff Sri G.S. Visharad died and Suit No.2 was already dismissed as withdrawn. It is necessary at this stage to mention that one more suit being Regular Suit No.25 of 1950 (O.O.S. No.2 of 1989) had been filed by Paramhans Ramachandra Das against Zahoor Ahmad and seven others. First five defendants were Muslims, residents of Ayodhya and were defendants No.1 to 5 in Suit No.1 also. Defendant No.6 was state of UP and defendant No.7 was Deputy Commissioner, Faizabad. Sunni Central Board of Waqfs was added as defendant No.8 in 1989. The plaint was almost verbatim reproduction of the plaint of Suit No.1. However, in Suit No.2, it was mentioned that notice under Section 80, C.P.C. had been given to defendants No.6 & 7 on 07.02.1950. Valuation was also same and reliefs claimed were also same. Boundaries of the 45 properties in dispute at the bottom of the plaint were also same. The suit was filed on 05.12.1950.

However, an application to get the said suit dismissed as withdrawn was filed by the plaintiff on 23.08.1990 which was allowed on 18.09.1990. It appears that Suit No.2 was filed only for the reason that before filing Suit No.1, notice under Section 80, C.P.C. had not been given. O.O.S. No.3 of 1989, Regular Suit No.26 of 1959, hereinafter referred to as Suit No.3 was filed by Nirmohi Akhara through its *mahant*. After the death of the original *mahant*, his disciple substituted him. Defendant No.1 in the suit was initially Babu Priya Datt Ram, who was appointed as receiver in proceedings under Section 145, Cr.P.C. Thereafter, the new receiver Jamuna Prasad was substituted in his place by order of court of October 1989. Defendants No.2 to 5 were state of UP, Deputy Commissioner, Faizabad, City Magistrate and S.P., Faizabad. Defendant No.6 was Phekku but after his death, he has been substituted by his sons. Defendant No.7 was Mohd. Faiq. Defendant No.8 was Mohd. Achhan Mian. Defendant No.11 Mohd. Farook was added vide order of court dated 03.12.1991. Defendant No.9 was UP Sunni Central Board of Waqfs, Lucknow added vide order of court dated 23.08.1989. One Umesh Chandra Pandey was later on impleaded as defendant No.10 on 28.01.1989 on his own application. The case of plaintiff Nirmohi Akhara was that for a very long time in Ayodhya, an ancient *math* and *akhara* of Ramanandi Varagis called Nirmohis existed which was a religious establishment of a public character. It was further pleaded that *Janmasthan* now commonly known as Janmabhoomi, the birthplace of Lord Ramachandra at the time of filing of the suit belonged and had always belonged to Nirmohi Akhara, who through its *mahant* and *sarbrahkar* had always been managing and receiving offerings made there in the form of money, etc. It was also claimed in para 3 of the plaint that *47 asthan* of Janmabhoomi was of ancient antiquity. A map of the property in dispute was also attached along with the plaint and the entire premises was claimed to be a temple. After the demolition on 06.12.1992, the plaint was amended. It was asserted that the main temple and other temples of Nirmohi Akhara were also demolished by some miscreants, who had no religion, caste or creed. It was also claimed in para 4-A that Nirmohi Akhara was the *panchyati math* of Ramanandi sect of Bairagis and as such was a religious denomination and the customs had been reduced in writing on 19.03.1949 by registered deed.

□

6

Ramjanmabhoomi Movement (1983-1992)

The idea of building a Rama temple in Ayodhya was reignited in 1983 when Dau Dayal Khanna, a veteran Congress leader from Uttar Pradesh, brought the issue of liberation of temples at Ayodhya, Mathura and Kashi (Varanasi) to the fore. Khanna used to be a minister in the cabinet of Chandrabhanu Gupta led Congress government in the state. Gupta was the third Chief Minister of Uttar Pradesh.

Khanna personally presented a resolution at a meeting in Muzaffarnagar (in Uttar Pradesh) in 1983, for rebuilding the three temples at Ayodhya, Mathura and Kashi. The meeting was organised by the Hindu Jagaran Manch.

Khanna reintroduced this resolution at a meeting organised by Vishwa Hindu Parishad (VHP) in New Delhi in 1984. This meeting was called *Dharma Sansad* (Parliament of Religions) and the saints from across the country were attending this meeting. The resolution was passed unanimously. It was followed by setting up of Shri Ramjanmabhoomi Mukti Yajna Samiti under the chairmanship of Mahanta Avaidyanath. Dau Dayal Khanna was appointed as the general secretary of this new body.

Shri Ramjanmabhoomi Mukti Yajna Samiti had been set up to launch the movement for building a magnificent temple at the birthplace of Lord Rama in Ayodhya. The first programme undertook by Samiti was to take out Shri Rama-Janaki Rath Yatra from Sitamarhi (Bihar) to Delhi on 25 September, 1984. Later on six more such *yatras* were taken out in the state of Uttar Pradesh from Vijayadashami in 1985. The response was tremendous.

On 1 February, 1986, the District Magistrate of then Faizabad (now Ayodhya) district ordered opening of the locks of Shri Ramjanmabhoomi on a plea filed by an advocate, Umeshchandra Pandey. In 1989, the High Court dismissed all the appeals filed against the order of opening the lock.

When the lock was opened, Shri Ramjanmabhoomi had a battered three-domed structure. The Samiti started planning for building a magnificent temple there. Shri Chandrakant Bhai Somapura from Karnavati (Ahmedabad) was selected as the architect for the proposed temple. According to the draft design finalised after several rounds of consultations, the proposed temple was to be two-storeyed. The temple would be constructed with sandstone from Bansi Pahadpur of Bharatpur district in Rajasthan. No iron would be used in the construction of this temple. Each storey would have 106 pillars, with a height of 16.5 ft on ground floor and 14.5ft on the first floor. Every storey would have 185 beams and they would also be made up of stone and maximum length of the beam would be 16ft. The temple would have a marble frame with wooden doors fitted for its main entrance.

To lay the foundation stone of the temple, an unprecedented campaign was taken at the national level. A small coupon with a picture of the proposed Rama temple on it was sold for ₹1.25 each to every individual who wanted to contribute in the construction of the Rama temple. This was accompanied by *shilapoojan* (worshipping of bricks) by groups of people collectively across the nation. Such ceremonies were held in homes, offices, public places, temples and wherever it was possible to do so.

These worshipped *shila* (bricks) were sent back to Ayodhya to be a part of the foundation of the proposed Rama temple. More than 2.75 lakh such bricks were sent, covering every nook and corner of the country.

On 10 November, 1989, the foundation stone of Rama temple was laid down by a Kameshwar *chaupal* near the main gate of the proposed temple. The *chaupal* belonged to a backward caste.

To construct the temple through efforts of the common people, the Samiti decided to organise *karseva*, a kind of voluntary contribution by working on the temple site. The decision to perform this *karseva* was taken on 23-24 June, 1990 at Haridwar (which was then part of Uttar Pradesh, as Uttarakhand had not come into existence at that time). The then Chief Minister Mulayam Singh announced he wouldn't let even a bird pass over the proposed site of *karseva*, which was the birthplace of Lord Rama.

In spite of crackdown of Uttar Pradesh police and airtight security, thousands of *karsevaks* reached Ayodhya and unfurled the saffron flags at three domes on 1 November, 1990. On 2 November, 1992 the government security personnel opened fire, killing several *karsevaks* in the narrow lanes and bylanes of Ayodhya. The official death toll in the incident was 18, while the unofficial death toll was much higher. Witnesses claimed that hundreds were killed. An online report in *India Today* report by Prabhash K Dutta on 30 October, 2019 recalled this gory incident. Titled 'Ayodhya: When Mulayam Singh Yadav ordered police firing on *karsevaks* heading to Babri Masjid', the report says: "Mulayam Singh Yadav was the Chief Minister of Uttar Pradesh in 1990, when the BJP, VHP and the RSS had given a call for *karseva* in Ayodhya. With *karsevaks* marching towards Babri Masjid, he ordered the police to open fire.

"... Though the campaign for a Rama temple in Ayodhya was underway since a 1986 resolution of the RSS Pratinidhi

Sabha, it gathered momentum after the then BJP president, L.K. Advani decided to lead a nationwide *rath yatra*.

"... VP Singh government was on shaky ground at the Centre due to infighting in the ruling Janata Dal. In Uttar Pradesh, Mulayam Singh Yadav of the same party was the Chief Minister. The Janata Dal was vehemently against the Ayodhya campaign by the RSS, the BJP and the VHP.

"'Let them try and enter Ayodhya. We will teach them the meaning of law. No *masjid* will be broken', Mulayam Singh Yadav had declared this in October 1990, opposing the *rath yatra* of L.K. Advani.

"L.K. Advani could not enter Ayodhya as he was arrested in Bihar by the Lalu Prasad government of the Janata Dal. But the Ayodhya campaign had seen a huge gathering of *karsevaks* (volunteers) in the Uttar Pradesh city.

"As they tried to march towards the Babri Masjid—intention not clearly declared—on October 30, a clash erupted between the *karsevaks* and the police. October 30 was the D-day of the *karseva*. The organisers—the VHP, the RSS and the BJP—wanted a Rama temple at the site of Babri Masjid but it was not yet clear what the *karsevaks* would do to the mosque.

"On the morning of October 30, the police had barricaded about 1.5 km-long pathway to the Babri Masjid. Ayodhya was in an unprecedented security cordon. Curfew had been imposed. Yet, *sadhus* and *karsevaks* marched towards the structure.

"By noon, police received orders from then Chief Minister Mulayam Singh Yadav to open fire at the *karsevaks*. The firing led to chaos and stampede. Police chased down the *karsevaks* in the streets of Ayodhya.

"Another round of clash erupted on November 2, when the *karsevaks* came back and resumed their march towards the Babri Masjid, adopting a different tactic.

"The *karsevaks,* comprising also of women and elderly people, would touch the feet of the security personnel deployed to prevent the demonstrators from marching ahead. Stunned by feet-touching gestures—two days after the firing incident—the security personnel would step back and the *karsevaks* would move forward to do a repeat.

"The security people saw through the tactic and warned them. The *karsevaks* would not be deterred. The security forces responded by opening fire the second time in three days.

"Many died in the clashes. Official records showed 17 deaths but the BJP put the death toll higher. Among the dead were Kothari brothers—Ram and Sharad—from Kolkata. They were seen atop the Babri Masjid on October 30, holding the saffron flag.

"Their bodies were found on November 2 in a lane near the Hanumangarhi temple, which is in the vicinity of the Ramjanmabhoomi-Babri Masjid site. It was alleged that police had dragged them out of a house and killed them.

"... In 2017, addressing his supporters on his 79th birthday, Mulayam Singh Yadav justified his order to open fire at *karsevaks*."

The massacre of *karsevaks* at Ayodhya had a huge fallout. The V.P. Singh government collapsed at the Centre. There was a 40 day *satyagraha* (peaceful protest to protect the truth) at Ayodhya by *karsevaks*. In April, 1991, Mulayam had to resign as Chief Minister.

When Chandrahsekhar replaced V.P. Singh as the Prime Minister, his emissaries convinced Vishwa Hindu Parishad and Babri Masjid Action Committee to start talking with each other on this issue. The key theme of the talks was: If it is proved that the disputed structure/Babri mosque has been constructed on Shri Ramjanmabhoomi by demolishing a temple, the Muslims would give up their claim over it. Both the parties agreed to submit their respective evidences in writing to the Minister of

State for Home Affairs by 22 December,1990 and who would, in turn, exchange the same between the parties concerned by 25 December, 1990. Both the parties would review these evidences and submit their comments to the Minister of State for Home Affairs by 6 January, 1991. Both the parties had to prepare their points of agreement and disagreement and send them to the parties concerned by 9 January, 1991. They met again on January 10. The discussions were held in Gujarat Bhawan in New Delhi.

It was agreed upon that experts from four categories: history, archaeology, revenue administration and law would analyse the available evidences. The experts met in two groups to study the evidences on 24 January, 1991. The Muslims' experts had belonged to history and archaeology and they submitted in writing, seeking another six weeks to study the evidences further. The Hindus' experts said they were ready to meet again as early as 5 February, 1991. The Muslims' experts in revenue and law did not attend this meeting. Another meeting was to be held on 25 January, 1991. The experts from Hindu side reached Gujarat Bhavan at 11 a.m. and waited till 12:45 but none of the Muslims' experts came. This sudden disappearance of the experts from Muslim side led to the breakdown in the talks.

Meanwhile, the Kalyan Singh-led Bharatiya Janata Party government in UP decided to acquire 2.77 acres of land surrounding the disputed structure on 10 October, 1991 for developing facilities for pilgrims. The acquisition was challenged by the Muslims in the High Court. The latter gave an interim order on 25 October, 1991 that Uttar Pradesh government could take possession of the acquired land but no *pucca* construction should be done there till the appeals are finally disposed off. The final hearing on the appeals was completed on 4 November, 1992 and the decision was kept reserved.

The tourism department of Uttar Pradesh government began the work of levelling the plot of 2.77 acres in April, 1992. Apart from this, the work of constructing an 80-feet road was also started alongside by the Public Works Department (PWD) to join Janmabhoomi to the National Highway No. 8 (Lucknow-Faizabad-Ayodhya-Gorakhpur Highway).

During the course of levelling the land, the workers came across a huge treasure of carved stone pieces of different shapes, sizes and designs in the south-eastern corner of the structure. These pieces were recovered from 12 feet under the surface on 18 June, 1992. They contained broken pieces of carved and designed stones. All those pieces are kept secured in Ayodhya Museum now. The archaeologists who inspected the site on July 2-3 arrived at a conclusion that they were the remnants of a temple pertaining to a style that was prevalent during the 12th century in north Bharat. The most prominent among these remnants included a spire, emblic myrobalan, decorative mesh, head portico, pillar bases, door segment, Shiva-Parvati figures, etc. A wide and sturdy wall of burnt bricks was also found underneath the disputed structure.

□

7

Demolition of Disputed Structure

In May 1992, a large number of saints and ascetics representing various religious sects of Hindus gathered at Ujjain in the state of Madhya Pradesh. They passed a resolution to start the next stage of *karseva* for the construction of a new and magnificent temple at the birthplace of Rama, i.e. Ramjanmabhoomi from the *shilanyas* site (where the foundation was laid earlier). A delegation of saints also met the then Prime Minister P.V. Narasimha Rao and apprised him of their resolve for the *karseva*. They requested him to carry on with the mediation with the representatives of Muslim groups or organisations objecting to the construction of Rama temple in Ayodhya.

Meanwhile the levelling of the 'disputed' site of 2.77 acres had also been started under the supervision of R.N. Srivastava, the then District Magistrate of Faizabad.

On 18 June, 1992 a new startling archaeological finding came to light during the process of levelling. According to *Ramjanmabhoomi Ayodhya: New Archeological Discoveries* (NAD; Sharma, Y.D., K.M Srivastava *et al.*, 1992):

"At a depth of about 12 feet from the ground level near the Ramjanmabhoomi temple, towards the south and beyond the fencing, a big hoard of beautifully carved buff sandstone pieces were located in a large pit, dug down below the old top level."

A careful study by a group of eight eminent archaeologists and historians found that all these objects are architectural members of a Hindu temple-complex of the 11th century CE.

The group comprised Dr. Y.D. Sharma, former Deputy Director-General, Archaeological Survey of India, Dr. K.M. Srivastava, former Director, Archaeological Survey of India, Dr. S.P. Gupta, former Director, Allahabad Museum, Prof. K.P. Nautiyal, Vice-Chancellor, Avadh University and former Head of the Ancient History and Archaeology Department, Garhwal University, Prof. B.R.Grover, former Director, Indian Council of Historical Research, Shri Devendra Swarup Agrawal and Dr. Sardindu Mukherji of the Delhi University, and Dr. (Mrs.) Sudha Malaya of Bhopal.

The experts who visited the site on behalf of the academic organisation, 'The Historians' Forum', on the 2nd and 3rd of July 1992, were unanimously of the view that the temple,.to which these fragments belong, is of the developed Nagara style of ancient temple architecture which was current in northern India during the latter part of the early medieval period, i.e. the period after 900 CE and before 1200 CE. The temples of this style are characterised by a distinctly imposing *shikhara*, which is a tall and tapering spire over the *garbha griha* or sanctum sanctorum, which houses the main deity.

There were more than forty sculptural and architectural remains. The finds included disjointed and broken image, *shikhara amalaka*, *Shikhara kala*, the capital, cornice, floral frieze, door-jamb and images of Vishnu's Incarnations. There is also a fragment of a stele embellished with the most significant sculptures of a number of Vaishnavite gods, viz. a *chakrapurusha*, i.e. a youthful male figure standing gracefully at an angle (*tribhanga*) and holding vertically in the palm of the right hand the characteristic wheel or *chakra* of Vishnu. Another image is that of Parshurama sitting cross-legged and holding a battle-axe in the left hand. Below him is the image of Balarama, the elder brother of Krishna, with a canopy of serpent-hoods and having a wine-cup in his hand. Still below him is the image of a mother goddess (Maitri-Devi), the bestower of all good luck and terracotta. Figurines belonging to the earlier periods, such as the Kushana (1st-3rd century) have also been found. These images belong to various Hindu gods and goddesses.

From July 4 to 18 July, 1992, Prof. B.R. Grover camped at Ayodhya, during the period when the ground acquired by the U.P. government was being levelled up. Towards the east and south of the Ramjanmabhoomi, he came across large floor-areas, in the pre-Islamic levels, which were carefully paved. During that period, Prof. Grover had released as many as three reports of his findings to the press which prompted the Historian's Forum to send two eminent field-archaeologists to examine the reported discoveries.

As the levelling work progressed, more evidences of a temple beneath the mosque began to surface. A 12 feet deep section also surfaced in the levelling. This was examined by former Director of ASI, Dr. K.M. Srivastava and Dr. S.P. Gupta. A huge ancient burnt-brick wall running north-south along the section was identified. Below it was another wall with distinct flooring of large bricks. There were brick debris and large pits which suggested destruction of a huge wall. Dr. Rakesh Tiwari, Director, U.P. State Archaeology, prepared a list of 263 artefacts belonging to a Hindu temple and stated to the court that these had been found at the site.

On July 9, the *karseva* started in Ayodhya and it carried on for around 17 days till July 26. The atmosphere of the country remained peaceful during these 17 days. In spite of the Central Government objecting to the *karseva*, the Bharatiya Janata Party-ruled U.P. government allowed it, but only in the undisputed area. The then Union Home Minister

S.B. Chavan asked the state govternment to stop the *karseva* with immediate effect. But it didn't.

Amidst the sacred hymn chanting by 1,400 Vedic Brahmins the construction of the foundation of proposed temple had begun. Vinay Katiyar and Vishwa Hindu Parishad leader Ashok Singhal were the first to initiate the *karseva*. Also witness to this were the saints of Ramjanmabhoomi Nyas, representatives of VHP besides two ministers of the U.P. government. The earth was first purified with the sprinkling of water from River Saryu on whose banks Ayodhya is situated. Vishwanath Vamdev, head of the Vedic Studies Department at Benaras Hindu University performed the Ganesh *puja* before the construction began. A galaxy of prominent personalities carried bricks and cement as a part of *karseva* to the construction site. Some of them were Rajmata Vijayaraje Scindia, Ashok Singhal, Acharya Giriraj Kishore, Mahant Nrityagopala Das, Paramhans Ramachandra Das, Mahant Avaidyanath, Uma Bharati, Sadhvi Ritambhara, Swami Vamdev, Acharya Dharmendra, Daudayal Khanna, Vishnu Hari Dalmia.

The *karseva* had started for construction on 100 ft long and 80 ft wide platform on which columns were supposed to be erected. This was supposed to be the entrance of the proposed temple. After that the sanctum sanctorum and a general assembly hall were to be constructed. The planning of foundation was done under the guidance of Roorkee Engineering College's former Vice-Chancellor and his team of five engineers.

Meanwhile, a petition had been filed in the Supreme Court to stop this *karseva*. The vacation judge, Justice M.N. Venkatachaliah asked the U.P. government about the details of the construction work. Justice Venkatachaliah had made it clear that that if any permanent structure was found to be constructed on disputed land, it will be demolished.

An interesting episode has been quoted by author

Hemant Sharma in his book, *Yudh mein Ayodhya* about Union Home Minister S.B. Chavan's visit to Ayodhya on 12 July, 1992 to inspect the nature of construction at the site. Chavan went to the sanctum sanctorum and performed *puja*. After that he asked, "Since I have visited the temple, now take me to the mosque." People there started laughing and told him that this is also the mosque.

On July 14, Chavan spelled out his government's stand in Rajya Sabha that even if *karseva* went on in Ayodhya, the government would not let anyone touch Babri mosque.

On 15 July, 1992 the Allahabad High Court put a stop on *karseva*. Meanwhile the Supreme Court gave direction to the U.P. government to submit an affidavit that no permanent structure was being built on the disputed area. The team that went to Ayodhya with Chavan gave the report that while the Babri mosque was intact, the construction going on there was certainly not temporary.

The lawyers representing the U.P. government had expressed their inability in giving details of the construction to the court as the *sadhus* (saints) of Ayodhya didn't let them go near the structure and hence they could not assess.

On July 18, the Faizabad administration expressed their inability in implementing court orders through force. On 20 July, 1992 the Faizabad Collector met leaders of VHP to discuss the implementation of the latest court orders. Chavan said in the Lok Sabha that they have an emergency plan as a solution.

The Supreme Court asked the U.P. government to reveal the nature of work going on in Ayodhya. It further said that if the state government would get the construction work stopped, the court would combine all cases and they would be heard by a large bench on daily basis so that the court could decide whether the temple could be built on the acquired land.

On July 23, the Prime Minister again appealed to stop the

construction, indicating that the government was willing to resolve the issue in stipulated time.

On 25 July, 1992 a representative of the Prime Minister met VHP leader Ashok Singhal with an assurance that the Prime Minister would not only personally handle the matter, but would also find a solution within three months by consulting both the parties. In response to this appeal, the construction work was stopped. However, the leaders of the VHP also indicated that the *karseva* could resume in the month of October-November, 1992, if a solution is not found within three months's deadline.

In September 1992, *Sri Rama padukapujan* (worshipping the footwear of Lord Rama) was organised in villages across the country. Another call was given to devotees to reach Ayodhya on Gita Jayanti (6 December, 1992).

Amidst all this, a group of 45 historians and archaeologists conducted a seminar at Ayodhya to examine the ASI's latest findings on the disputed site. Meenakshi Jain has given detailed account of this seminar in her book *Rama and Ayodhya* (pp. 187). According to Jain, during the exploration trip, R.C. Agarwala, former Director of Department of Archaeology and Museums, Government of Jaipur, discovered a letter 'Shri' written in Nagari script. It was found to be written on a black stone pillar fixed on the left-hand outer wall of the main entrance of the Babri mosque. It was found to be of 11th-12th centuries. Another finding was on the eastern boundary wall of the *masjid*. It was found that this was built on the plinth of the temple.

"Dr. S.R. Rao, advisor on Marine Archaeology at the Institute of Oceanography, Goa, also came upon a large piece of stone decorated with floral motifs fixed below the southern dome on the eastern wall of the structure"(*BJP Today*, 1-15 February 1993: 13-17).

On 6 December, 1992, more than 1.5 lakh Hindus

reached Ayodhya for the symbolic *karseva*. The efforts of the state administration and paramilitary forces to stop people from coming to the place where Lord Rama was born (Ramjanmasthan) proved futile.

The forces deployed in and around Ayodhya included 35 companies of Provincial Armed Constabulary (PAC), 195 companies of paramilitary forces, four companies of CRPF, 15 tear gas squads, 15 police inspectors, 30 police sub-inspectors and 2,300 police constables. Both political and religious leaders present there were addressing the crowd since morning. Although it started like a public rally but within a couple of hours the crowd gradually grew restless and started raising slogans.

In spite of clear instructions by these leaders that the disputed structure shouldn't be disturbed, devotees of Lord Rama grew even more impatient. The crowd ripped through the heavy barricades which had been put up around Babri structure for its safety. Riding high on the passion, a group of *karsevaks* (volunteers performing *karseva*) climbed up the three-domed structure and brought it down.

The entire structure made from mud and chalk was levelled by the crowd with axes, hammers, and grappling hooks. Within next five hours, the *karsevaks* pulled down the disputed structure. A deity of Sri Ram Lalla was installed at a flat platform. The place was enclosed by a boundary wall made of bricks and a canopy was also erected for the protection of the deity. The *puja* also had continued there. Incidentally many remnants of a Hindu temple were recovered from the debris of the demolished Babri structure.

After this incident, two first information reports (FIRs) were filed at the Ramjanmabhoomi police station. One of the FIRs was lodged by the Station House Officer (SHO) of this police station, Priyamvada Nath Shukla. This FIR was registered against unknown *karsevaks* at 17:15 hrs on

06-12-1992. The second FIR was lodged by *chowki* in-charge Ganga Prasad Tiwari. The inquiry reports were submitted to Circle Officer of Inayat Nagar, R.P. Tandon. This inquiry report was later given to the Central Bureau of Investigation also.

The second FIR lodged by Tiwari invoked Section 153A, 153B, 505 of the Indian Penal Code. It alleged the time of occurrence of the demolition as 10 a.m. on 6 December, 1992. Tiwari named the following prominent leaders in this FIR:

1. Ashok Singhal
2. Giriraj Kishore
3. L.K. Advani
4. Murli Manohar Joshi
5. Vishnu Hari Dalmia
6. Vinay Katiyar
7. Uma Bharati
8. Sadhvi Ritambhara

On the basis of this FIR, L.K. Advani, Vishnu Hari Dalmia, Ashok Singhal, Murli Manohar Joshi, Uma Bharati and Vinay Katiyar were arrested on 8 December, 1992 but they were released on 10 January, 1993 due to lack of evidence.

Besides the above-mentioned two FIRs related to demolition of disputed structure, 46 other FIRs with respect to cognisable offences and one FIR relating to non-cognisable offences, (all relating to offences committed against mediapersons who were recording the occurrence of demolition of the disputed structure and whose video cameras, etc., were allegedly snatched away or claimed to have been broken/stolen/robbed of etc.) were also lodged at Ramjanmabhoomi police station on 6 December, 1992.

In wake of the demolition, U.P. Chief Minister Kalyan Singh resigned in the evening. He boldly took the responsibility for issuing written orders that security forces would not resort to firing against the *karsevaks*.

On 10 December, 1992 the investigation regarding

one of the main cases lodged after the demolition of the Babri structure was handed over to the Central Bureau of Investigation. On the same day, the Central Government declared five organisations unlawful in wake of the December 6 incident in Ayodhya. These organisations were Rashtriya Swayamsevak Sangh, Vishwa Hindu Parishad, Bajrang Dal, Isalmi Sevak Sangh and Jamait-e-Islami. The ban was imposed under Unlawful Activities (Prevention) Act, 1967.

While most of the non-BJP parties welcomed this move, the Bharatiya Janata Party called it unfortunate and backed RSS, VHP and the Bajrang Dal. The RSS also termed this ban as unfortunate and malafide. On 15 December, 1992, the Central Government dismissed the BJP governments in Himachal Pradesh, Rajasthan and Madhya Pradesh in wake of the demolition of Babri mosque under Article 356 of the Constitution of India.

On 16 December, 1992 Advani along with five other leaders were arrested and sent to Lalitpur jail in U.P. The U.P. government handed over the FIR to a special court in Lalitpur.

Around 10 days later, the Central Government decided to acquire the land at the disputed site as well as around it.

On a petition seeking right to perform puja, the Allahabad High Court granted on 1 January, 1993, the right to perform puja and Darshan. The puja has been going on there since then without any break.

On 7 January, 1993, the Central Government acquired 67.7 acre land in Ramjanmabhoomi-Babri mosque campus through an ordinance titled 'Acquisition of Certain Area at Ayodhya Ordinance, No. 8.' (Details are in Chapter-8)

On 7 January, 1993 the President of India sent a reference to the Supreme Court, under Article 143(1) of the Constitution for consideration and opinion, the following question: Chapter-8

"Whether a Hindu temple or any Hindu religious structure existed prior to the construction of the Ramjanmabhoomi-Babri Masjid (including the premises of the inner and outer courtyards of such structure) in the area on which the structure stood?"

From 1993 to 2002, legal proceedings had started against several leaders associated with the Ramjanmabhoomi movement for their alleged role in demolition of the Babri mosque.

By 2002, the Ramjanmabhoomi movement was ready to enter the next stage. In February 2002, the Vishwa Hindu Parishad announced a new deadline of 15 March, 2002 to start construction of the Rama temple in Ayodhya.

A large number of *karsevaks* started gathering in Ayodhya. They came from all over the country. A contingent of *karsevaks* had also come from Godhara in Gujarat. When they were going back to their homes on *Sabarmati Express* train, there was an attack on their compartment S-6. Fifty-eight *karsevaks* were burnt alive. Gujarat witnessed widespread riots in reaction to this incident, leading to more than 1,000 deaths in the state.

In April 2002, a three-judge bench of High Court started hearing to determine the ownership of land.

The HC ordered the Archaeological Survey of India (ASI) to excavate the site to determine whether it had a temple earlier.

To find out the direct answer to the presidential special reference, in August 2002, the said bench ordered Ground Penetrating Radar Survey (GPRS) of the site.

In January 2003, a search with a ground-penetrating radar was conducted and Claude Robillard, a Canadian and the chief geophysicist for this project, stated the following:

"There is some structure under the mosque. The structure was ranging from 0.5 to 5.5 metres in depth that could be associated with ancient and contemporaneous structures, such

as pillars, foundation walls, slab flooring, extending over a large portion of the site.

"There are some anomalies found underneath the site relating to some archaeological features. You might associate them (the anomalies) with pillars, or floors, or concrete floors, wall foundation or something. These anomalies could be associated with archaeological features."

This proved scientifically that the Babri structure was not built on barren or vacant land as claimed by Muslims in their civil suit filed in December 1961, before the Civil Judge of Faizabad.

The expert was also of the opinion that to verify the GPRS report, scientific excavation should be carried out.

In 2003, the High Court ordered the ASI to excavate the site scientifically and verify the GPRS report. The excavation was conducted in the presence of two observers appointed by the court (two Additional District Judges of Faizabad). The parties concerned, their counsels, their experts/representatives were permitted to remain present during excavation. To maintain impartiality, it was ordered that 40 per cent of the labour would be Muslims. The archaeologists also reported evidence of a large structure pre-existing the Babri Masjid. A team of 131 labourers, including 52 Muslims was engaged in the excavations. On 11 June, 2003 the ASI issued an interim report that only listed the findings of the period between 22 May and 6 June, 2003. In August 2003, the ASI handed a 574-page report to the Lucknow bench of the Allahabad High Court. Minute-to-minute videography and still photography of excavation were duly done by the ASI.

Here is a summary of the ASI report:

Summary of Excavation Report by Archaeological Department

On the basis of the indication found about certain geological imponderables in the GPR conducted by Tojo

Vikas International, the Archaeological Survey of India (ASI) has conducted the excacation in the said premises from 12 March, 2003 to 7 August, 2003 as per the directives of the Hon'ble Lucknow High Court. Eighty-two trenches were dug on all sides of the make-shift temple of Shri Ram Lalla. The geological imponderables were found to be true and pillar-bases, architectural structures, floorings and remnants of other bases were secured. Some other trenches also were dug out apart from these 82 trenches, whereby their total number worked to about 90 trenches. The summary of this report regarding the excavation activities is as follows:

Indication was found of the inhabitation of those most ancient people, who were using the North Black Polished Earthern Wares (NBPW) in the premises of the disputed site in Ayodhya. Although no indication was found about any structural activities before the first millennia, B.C., even then the remnants of the terra-cotta idols, especially those of the goddesses, beads of terra-cottas and glass, wheels and trenches prepared for worship, etc. were found. On the basis of earthern wares with brown, black and red polish, a speciality of those periods gets manifested and that is earthern architecture. One round coin with unclear Brahmi script of Ashokan period engraved on it, was also found.

Scientifically this period is considered to be between 1000 years B.C. to A.D. 300. The second layer of cultural activities comes of Shung period (second and first century B.C.). Matru Goddess of terra-cotta, earthern idols of humans and animals, beads, hair-pins and excavators, etc. were found, which belong to this period. The remnants of earthen wares with black, brown and red polish were also found. The beginning of architectural sculpture was seen, which is quite evident from the structures of stone and burnt brickwork.

After the Shung period, there are indications of cultural supremacy of Kushan period (first and second centuries

A.D.). Human and animal images of terra-cotta, remnants of shrines, beads, hair-pins, broken pieces of bangles, remnants of earthern wares with red polish and collyrium sticks are the specialities of this period.

No proof of qualitative change in the architectural activities after the advent of the Gupta period (fourth to sixth century A.D.) was found, although this period is known for its classical arts. Things like specific figures of terra-cotta and one copper coin with Shri Chandra (Gupta) and other signs thereon represent this era.

Architectural activities continued during the post-Gupta-Rajput period (seventh and tenth centuries A.D.), especially preparation of burnt bricks has been the speciality of this period. A round altar (shrine) made up of bricks indicates the act of worship for the first time. Outwardly it is circular, but internally it is square and it has its door on the east. Although this construction is old and dilapidated, its northern wall has still a *prannali* (water chute), which has been the unique speciality of the temples of the Ganga-Yamuna plains.

Thereon, a massive construction was done on this site during the early medieval period (eleventh to twelfth centuries A.D.), which was 50 metres in length north-south. But it appears that this construction was shortlived. Of the 50, only four pillar-bases have been found during the excavation, the flooring of which are prepared from the brick-dust. On the remnants of the above construction, one more large structure has been built in three phases and its three floorings came before us.

The foliage and other decorative elements have been re-used, which are cut with the stencils, are found in the first construction and thus a massive structure or memorial was built. wherein there were single pillared or twin-pillared cells that are quite different from the residential blocks. This construction presents the proofs of the constructions that are used for the common people. This remained there for a long period—upto the central Sultan level (twelfth to sixteenth centuries A.D.). Right above this construction, the disputed structure (so-called Babri Masjid) was constructed in the beginning of the sixteenth century. Ample proofs have been found right below the disputed structure, wherefrom it is proved that there was a huge and wider construction, which was 50 metres in length (north-south) and 30 metres in east-west. About fifty pillar-bases have been found in the excavation, which are made up of bricks with concrete coating and stones placed on them.

These pillar-bases in the north-south region also give the indication that there was a lengthy huge wall, which could be excavated only upto 50 metres at this time. Centre of the central cell of the disputed structure is in the centre of the old wall. This wall could not be dug out fully because there is the make-shift temple of Shri Ram Lalla thereon. This area is a 15 x 15 platform. There is a round lower place in its east, which is in a hollow ditch constructed in bricks and here something, perhaps lamps, were offered to the adorable gods. The lamps made up of terra-cotta have been found in various trenches and they were in ample numbers in G-2 trench. From this the above fact stands confirmed.

The pieces of shining earthern wares, which remained there for a long time thereafter, and shining tiles have been found, which perhaps might have been used in the original construction. The pieces of silicon and china clay have been found in a very scant quantity. Animal bones belonging to different periods have been found at various levels. Remnants of human skeletons have also been found in the trenches in the north-south region, which belong to very late times. These graves are in the debris of the disputed structure and suppressed under the upper deposits of the debris.

Thus, it is found that from the remnants of various

constructional structures belonging from the Shung period to Gupta period, it has not become very clear as to which work were they being used for. It is worth mentionable here that no residential remnants were found at the said site that belonged only to Gupta period and further post-Mughal periods; and only debris or filling materials were found in the constructional layers, which might have been taken from the surrounding areas and used in levelling of the ground. As a result of this, earthern idols, terra-cotta and other materials belonging to most earlier period (NBPW) and Kushan period were found mixed in the recent debris. Thus it is concluded that the portion below the disputed structure was meant for the use of the common people.

This was going on from most earlier period to Mughal period without any impedance. The disputed structure (the so-called Babri Masjid) was built during Mughal period, which was in a limited area only and there was people's inhabitation all around it—its proofs are found in the form of archaeological materials like earthern wares, etc. There was a lack of residential constructions at the disputed site prior to Mughal period—such as deep wells, gutters, fire-places or ovens are totally missing. From this it is revealed that the said disputed site has not been used for residential purposes from Gupta period through to early medieval Rajput period and further upto medieval Sultan period and that it was in the use of the common people only.

The articles found in the said premises give indication of the mid-thirteenth century B.C. (1250 + or – 130 B.C.) on the basis of carbon-14 time determination tests; the lowest debris over the natural soil represents upto NBPW. Thus it is found that the most ancient remnants pertain to thirteenth century B.C. It has been testified according to carbon-14 test as 910 + or – 100 B.C. and 880 + or – 100 B.C. These remnants have been found in G-7 trench. As per the Radio-Carbon Time

Determination System also, they have been verified as 780 + or – 80 B.C., 530 + or – 530 70 B.C. and 320 + or – 80 B.C. These time determinations and NBPW remnants found in the said premises are considered to be pertaining to 600 B.C. to 300 B.C. and the ancient period goes back upto 1,000 B.C. Though proofs of NBPW evidences are not found, but the indication of human activities are found upto 13th century B.C., which has been verified even as per the scientific time-determination system.

In July, 2005, Islamic terrorists attacked the heavily guarded Ramjanmabhoomi-Babri mosque complex. The terror attack on July 5 left two locals dead. Seven paramilitary personnel were injured. Five suspected JeM terrorists were eliminated by security forces in retaliatory action.

Five persons were arrested by the U.P. police for involvement in this attack—Irfan, Ashiq Iqbal *alias* Farooque, Shakeel Ahmed, Mohammad Naseem and Mohammad Aziz. Five accused were arrested for conspiracy and providing logistic and material help to terror suspects. A special court in Allahabad sentenced four out of five accused to life-term imprisonment in June 2019.

In 2010, Allahabad High Court gave its verdict on the four petitions which had been clubbed together in this case. The court ordered to divide the disputed land into three parts with one-third each being given to Sri Ram Lalla, Sunni Central Waqf Board and Nirmohi Akhara. At least two of the aggrieved parties approached the Supreme Court against this verdict in December 2010 and the Supreme Court stayed the division of disputed land into three parts. The Supreme Court delivered a historic verdict in this case after a long wait in November 2019.

□

8

The Journey through Courts

The dispute related to the Rama temple in Ayodhya was the longest pending case in Indian courts. The first documentary evidence available regarding a dispute about the site dates back to 1858. In a report dated 28 November, 1858, the police-incharge of Oudh (Avadh) police station, *Thanedar* Sheetal Dubey, has mentioned about the worship in the middle of the mosque at the birthplace of Lord Rama. It was carried out by a Nihang Sikh Fakir Khalsa. This Nihang Sikh was from Punjab and he was accompanied by around 25 Sikhs, according to Dubey's report.

Meenakshi Jain has given a detailed account of the legal disputes in *Rama and Ayodhya*:

"Two days after the Nihang Sikh had begun worship in the middle of the *janmasthana* (birthplace) mosque, one Muhammad Asghar made a presentation (case number 884, Muhalla Kot Ramachandra, Ayodhya) to the British government seeking its intervention. Asghar was the *khattib* and *muezzin* of Babri mosque."

Supreme Court advocate Virag Gupta summed up this legal journey in the compendium, *Ayodhya's Rama Temple in Courts:* "In 1885, a civil suit was filed before the Council. After independence, the first suit was filed by Sri G.S. Visharad (Gopal Singh Visharad) of Hindu Mahasabha, claiming the right to pray in 1950. A subsequent suit was filed by Paramhans

Ramachandra Das against Zahoor Ahmed and seven other defendants. These seven defendants included five Muslim residents of Ayodhya, the state government of Uttar Pradesh and the Deputy Commissioner of Ayodhya. The Sunni Central Board was added as defendant No. 8 in 1989. In 1959, a third suit was filed by the Nirmohi Akhara through their *mahant*, claiming rights of management of temple. The fourth suit filed in 1961 was by the Sunni Central Board of Waqfs for removal of idols from the Babri mosque . In 1989, fifth suit was filed by Bhagwan Sri Ram Birajman and former judge of Allahabad High Court, Sri Deoki Nandan Agarwala, for construction of Rama temple. These claims and suits were transferred to Allahabad High Court in 1989 for early adjudication. These civil suits were decided by the Allahabad High Court in 2010."

The main disputed land in Ayodhya was approximately 2.77 acres. The Central Government had acquired the entire disputed land through 'The Acquisition of Certain Area at Ayodhya Act, 1993'.

However, the judgement of the Allahabad High Court (in *Gopal Singh Visharad v. Zahoor Ahmad, 2010 SCC Online All 1934*) ordered division of land into three equal parts to Ram Lalla, Nirmohi Akhara and the Sunni Waqf Board.

The judgement of Allahabad High Court was given by three judges: Justice Dharam Veer Sharma, Justice Sudhir Agarwal and Justice S.U. Khan. (Justice Sharma had asked the entire disputed site to be given to the Hindus in his judgement.) The Supreme Court ordered a stay on this judgement in 2011 as it had decided to hear appeals against this judgement.

Following are some of the important findings of the Allahabad High Court in its judgement regarding the 'birthplace' of Lord Rama at the disputed site:

Justice Dharam Veer Sharma

"The aforesaid assertions corroborate that a Hindu

temple used to exist at the birthplace of Lord Rama at Ramkot. *Encyclopaedia Britannica,* India, by Surgeon J.A. Balfour, *gazetteer* of P. Carnegy and other *gazetteers,* reveal the location of Babri mosque as the site of Ramjanmabhoomi and corroborate the version of William Finch that the pilgrims were offering prayers with a belief that the site was the birthplace of Lord Rama. Hans Bakker in his research work also corroborated the historical version. He also consulted religious books of Hindus and other historical books. I have already referred to important extracts of his thesis on the subject. Thus, from the material on record it transpires that the site used to be a temple on Ramjanmabhoomi which was reconstructed in 12th century and the same was demolished. A.S.I. also confirms ruins of 12th-century temple. Even the debris of the Babri mosque which were collected on 6.12.1992 proves the existence of Ramjanmabhoomi temple which was considered as the birthspot of Lord Rama. Fourteen kasauti pillars were taken from the old temple and were used in the construction of the mosque by Muslims on which images of Hindu gods and goddesses were engraved. Sita-ki-Rasoi and *charanpaduka* were identified by Hans Bakker."

Justice Sudhir Agarwal

"It is declared that the area covered by the central dome of the three-domed structure, i.e. the disputed structure being the deity of Bhagwan Ramjanmasthan and place of birth of Lord Rama as per faith and belief of the Hindus, belong to plaintiffs (Suit-5) and shall not be obstructed or interfered in any manner by the defendants.

"... We are satisfied and hold that the place of birth as believed and worshipped by Hindus is the area covered under the central dome of three-domed structure, i.e. the disputed structure, in the inner courtyard of the premises in dispute."

Presidential Reference of 1993

In 1993, the Central Government sent a reference through the President of India to the Supreme Court of India seeking its opinion on whether a Hindu temple or any Hindu religious structure existed prior to the construction of the Babri structure on the disputed site in 1993. A five-judge constitutional bench of the Supreme Court headed by Chief Justice M. Venkatachaliah in 1994, respectfully declined to answer the reference. Here is the text of this 'Special Reference'.

Special Reference

1. Whereas a dispute has arisen whether a Hindu temple or any Hindu religious structure existed prior to the construction of the structure (including the premises of the inner and outer courtyards of such structure, commonly known as the Ramjanmabhoomi-Babri Masjid, in the area in which the structure stood in village, Kot Ramachandra in Ayodhya, in Pargana Haveli Avadh, in *tehsil* Faizabad Sadar, in the district of Faizabad of the state of Uttar Pradesh;
2. And whereas the said area is located in Revenue Plot Nos. 159 and 160 in the said village, Kot Ramachandra;
3. And whereas the said dispute has affected the maintenance of public order and harmony between different communities in the country;
4. And whereas the aforesaid area vests in the Central Government by virtue of the Acquisition of Certain Area at Ayodhya Ordinance, 1993;
5. And whereas notwithstanding the vesting of the aforesaid area in the Central Government under the said ordinance, the Central Government proposes to settle the said dispute after obtaining the opinion of

the Supreme Court of India and in terms of the said opinion;

6. And whereas in view of what has been herein before stated, it appears to me that the question hereinafter set out has arisen and is of such a nature and of such public importance that it is expedient to obtain the opinion of the Supreme Court of India thereon;

7. Now, therefore, in exercise of the powers conferred upon me by clause (1) of Article 143 of the Constitution of India, I, Shankar Dayal Sharma, President of India, hereby refer the following question to the Supreme Court of India for consideration and opinion thereon, namely:

   Whether a Hindu temple or any Hindu religious structure existed prior to the construction of the Ramjanmabhoomi-Babri Masjid (including the premises of the inner and outer courtyards of such structure) in the area on which the structure stood?

Sd/-

President of India

New Delhi;
Dated 7th January, 1993

In *M. Ismail Faruqui (Dr) v. Union of India, (1994) 6 SCC 360*, Supreme Court declined to answer the above and said:

"(11) Consequently, the Special Reference No. 1 of 1993 [Ed. : For Order dated 27 January, 1993 of the present Bench on the Reference *see* (1993) 1 SCC 642] made by the President of India under Article 143(1) of the Constitution of India is superfluous and unnecessary and does not require to be answered. For this reason, we very respectfully decline to answer it and return the same."

According to Virag Gupta, "It is often said that a Rama temple at Ayodhya will open a Pandora's box of claims. However, the Parliament in 1991 enacted the Places of Worship (Special Provisions) Act, 1991 to protect religious structures. Made by the Narasimha Rao government, the law prohibited changing the nature of any religious structure. Interestingly, this new law also amended the S.8 of Representation of People's Act, 1951. It said that the nature of a structure will remain as it was on August 15, 1947. Importantly, Ramjanmabhoomi/Babri mosque was excluded by this law."

Places of Worship (Special Provisions) Act, 1991

[Act 42 of 1991]

[18th September, 1991]

An Act to prohibit conversion of any place of worship and to provide for the maintenance of the religious character of any place of worship as it existed on the 15th day of August, 1947, and for matters connected therewith or incidental thereto.

Be it enacted by Parliament in the Forty-second Year of the Republic of India as follows:

PLACES OF WORSHIP (SPECIAL PROVISIONS) ACT, 1991

Section 1. Short title, extent and commencement

1. Short title, extent and commencement

(1) This Act may be called the Places of Worship (Special Provisions) Act, 1991.

(2) It extends to the whole of India except the state of Jammu & Kashmir.

(3) The provisions of Sections 3, 6 and 8 shall come into force at once and the remaining provisions of this Act shall be deemed to have come into force on the 11th day of July, 1991.

PLACES OF WORSHIP (SPECIAL PROVISIONS) ACT, 1991

Section 2. Definitions

2. Definitions

In this Act, unless the context otherwise requires,

(a) "commencement of this Act" means the commencement of this Act on the 11th day of July, 1991;

(b) "conversion", with its grammatical variations, includes alteration or change of whatever nature;

(c) "place of worship" means a temple, mosque, *gurudwara*, church, monastery or any other place of public religious worship of any religious denomination or any section thereof, by whatever name called.

PLACES OF WORSHIP (SPECIAL PROVISIONS) ACT, 1991

Section 3. Bar on conversion of places of worship

No person shall convert any place of worship of any religious denomination or any section thereof into a place of worship of a different section of the same religious denomination or of a different religious denomination or any section thereof.

PLACES OF WORSHIP (SPECIAL PROVISIONS) ACT, 1991

Section 4. Declaration as to the religious character of certain places of worship and bar of jurisdiction of courts, etc.

4. Declaration as to the religious character of certain places of worship and bar of jurisdiction of courts, etc.

(1) It is hereby declared that the religious character of a place of worship existing on the 15th day of August, 1947 shall continue to be the same as it existed on that day.

(2) If, on the commencement of this Act, any suit, appeal or other proceeding with respect to the conversion of the religious character of any place of worship, existing on the 15th day of August, 1947, is pending before any court, tribunal or other authority, the same shall abate, and no suit, appeal or other proceeding with respect to any such matter shall lie on or after such commencement in any court, tribunal or other authority:

Provided that if any suit, appeal or other proceeding, instituted or filed on the ground that conversion has taken place in the religious character of any such place after the 15th day of August, 1947, is pending on the commencement of this Act, such suit, appeal or other proceeding shall not so abate and every such suit, appeal or other proceeding shall be disposed of in accordance with the provisions of sub-section (1).

(3) Nothing contained in sub-section (1) and sub-section (2) shall apply to,

(a) any place of worship referred to in the sub-sections which is an ancient and historical monument or an archaeological site or remains covered by the Ancient Monuments and Archaeological Sites and Remains Act,

1958 (24 of 1958) or any other law for the time being in force;

(b) any suit, appeal or other proceeding, with respect to any matter referred to in sub-section (2), finally decided, settled or disposed of by a court, tribunal or other authority before the commencement of this Act;

(c) any dispute with respect to any such matter settled by the parties amongst themselves before such commencement;

(d) any conversion of any such place effected before such commencement by acquiescence;

(e) any conversion of any such place effected before such commencement which is not liable to be challenged in any court, tribunal or other authority being barred by limitation under any law for the time being in force.

5. Act not to apply to Ramjanmabhoomi-Babri Masjid. Nothing contained in this Act shall apply to the place or place of worship commonly known as Ramjanmabhoomi-Babri Masjid situated in Ayodhya in the state of Uttar Pradesh and to any suit, appeal or other proceeding relating to the said place or place of worship.

6. **Punishment for contravention of Section 3**

(1) Whoever contravenes the provisions of Section 3 shall be punishable with imprisonment for a term which may extend to three years and shall also be liable to a fine.

(2) Whoever attempts to commit any offence punishable under sub-section (1) or to cause

such offence to be committed and in such attempt does any act towards the commission of the offence shall be punishable with the punishment provided for the offence.

(3) Whoever abets, or is a party to a criminal conspiracy to commit, an offence punishable under sub-section (1) shall, whether such offence be or be not committed in consequences of such abetment or in pursuance of such criminal conspiracy, and notwithstanding anything contained in Section 116 of the Indian Penal Code, be punishable with the punishment provided for the offence.

PLACES OF WORSHIP (SPECIAL PROVISIONS) ACT, 1991

Section 7. Act to override other enactments

The provisions of this Act shall have effect notwithstanding anything inconsistent therewith contained in any other law for the time being in force or any instrument having effect by virtue of any law other than this Act.

PLACES OF WORSHIP (SPECIAL PROVISIONS) ACT, 1991

Section 8. Amendment of Act 43 of 1951

8. Amendment of Act 43 of 1951[1] [Repealed]

Ed. The repeal by this Act of any enactment shall not affect any other enactment in which the repealed enactment has been applied, incorporated or referred to.

1. Prior to repeal by Act 30 of 2001, Section 8 read as:
    1. Amendment of Act 43 of 1951—In Section 8 of the Representation of the People's Act, 1951, in sub-section (1),—

(a) in clause (i), the word 'or' shall be inserted at the end;

(b) after clause (i), as so amended, the following clause shall be inserted, namely: "(j) Section 6 (offence of conversion of a place of worship) of the Places of Worship (Special Provisions) Act, 1991."

1. Repealed by Act 30 of 2001, Section 2 and Schedule I.

Acquisition of Land by Centre:

After the demolition of Babri mosque on 6 December, 1992 by *karsevaks*, the Congress government at the Centre acquired the disputed land in Ayodhya through an ordinance that later came to be known as 'The Acquisition of Certain Area at Ayodhya Act, 1993'.

The state of Uttar Pradesh was under President's Rule. According to Virag Gupta, "As per constitutional provisions, 'Land' is a matter of State List as Entry No. 18 and Entry No. 42 of Concurrent List is 'Acquisition and requisitioning of property', through which the Central Government had the power to acquire the land. After acquisition, the Central Government is owner of the land, though there are certain restrictions and status quo on disputed site of 2.77 acres of land."

The Acquisition of Certain Area at Ayodhya Act, 1993

(No. 33 of 1993, dt. 3rd April, 1993)

An Act to provide for the acquisition of a certain area at Ayodhya and for matters connected therewith or incidental thereto.

Whereas there has been a long-standing dispute relating to the structure (including the premises of the inner and outer courtyards of such structure), commonly known as the Ramjanmabhoomi-Babri Masjid, situated in village Kot Ramachandra in Ayodhya, in Pargana Haveli, Avadh, in *tehsil*,

Faizabad Sadar, in the district of Faizabad of the state of Uttar Pradesh;

And whereas the said dispute has affected the maintenance of public order and harmony between different communities in the country;

And whereas it is necessary to maintain public order and to promote communal harmony and the spirit of common brotherhood amongst the people of India;

And whereas with a view to achieving the aforesaid objectives, it is necessary to acquire certain areas in Ayodhya;

Be it enacted by Parliament in the Forty-fourth Year of the Republic of India as follows:

I
PRELIMINARY

1. Short title and commencement

(1) This Act may be called the Acquisition of Certain Area at Ayodhya Act, 1993.

(2) It shall be deemed to have come into force on the 7th day of January, 1993.

2. Definitions

In this Act unless the context otherwise requires,

(a) 'area' means the area (including all the buildings, structures or other properties comprised therein) specified in the Schedule;

(b) 'authorised person' means a person or body of persons or trustees of any trust authorised by the Central Government under Section 7;

(c) 'Claims Commissioner' means the Claims Commissioner appointed under sub-section (2) of Section 8;

(d) 'prescribed' means prescribed by rules made under this Act.

II

ACQUISITION OF THE AREA IN AYODHYA

3. Acquisition of rights in respect of certain area

On and from the commencement of this Act, the right, title and interest in relation to the area shall, by virtue of this Act, stand transferred to, and vest in, the Central Government.

4. General effect of vesting

(1) The area shall be deemed to include all assets, rights, leaseholds, powers, authority and privileges and all property, movable and immovable, including lands, buildings, structures, shops of whatever nature or other properties and all other rights and interests in, or arising out of, such properties as were immediately before the commencement of this Act in the ownership, possession, power or control of any person or the state government of Uttar Pradesh, as the case may be, and all registers, maps, plans, drawings and other documents of whatever nature relating thereto.

(2) All properties aforesaid which have vested in the Central Government under Section 3 shall, by force of such vesting, be freed and discharged from any trust, obligation, mortgage, charge, lien and all other encumbrances affecting them and any attachment, injunction, decree or order of any court or tribunal or other authority restricting the use of such properties in any manner or appointing any receiver in respect of the whole or any part of such properties shall cease to have any effect.

(3) If, on the commencement of this Act, any suit, appeal or other proceeding in respect of the right, title and interest relating to any property

which has vested in the Central Government under Section 3, is pending before any court, tribunal or other authority, the same shall abate.

5. **Duty of person or state government in-charge of the management of the area to deliver all assets, etc.**

(1) The Central Government may take all necessary steps to secure possession of the area which is vested in that government under Section 3.

(2) On the vesting of the area in the Central Government under Section 3, the person or state government of Uttar Pradesh, as the case may be, in-charge of the management of the area immediately before such vesting shall be bound to deliver to the Central Government or the authorised person, all assets, registers and other documents in their custody relating to such vesting or where it is not practicable to deliver such registers or documents, the copies of such registers or documents authenticated in the prescribed manner.

6. **Power of Central Government to direct vesting of the area in another authority or body or trust**

(1) Notwithstanding anything contained in Sections 3, 4, 5 and 7, the Central Government may, if it is satisfied that any authority or other body, or trustees of any trust, set up on or after the commencement of this Act is or are willing to comply with such terms and conditions as that government may think fit to impose, direct by notification in the Official Gazette, that the right, title and interest or any of them in relation to the area or any part thereof, instead of continuing to vest in the Central Government, vest in that

authority or body or trustees of that trust either on the date of the notification or on such later date as may be specified in the notification.

(2) When any right, title and interest in relation to the area or part thereof vest in the authority or body or trustees referred to in sub-section (1), such rights of the Central Government in relation to such area or part thereof, shall, on and from the date of such vesting, be deemed to have become the rights of that authority or body or trustees of that trust.

(3) The provisions of Sections 4, 5, 7 and 11 shall, so far as may be, apply in relation to such authority or body or trustees as they apply in relation to the Central Government and for this purpose, references therein to the Central Government shall be construed as references to such authority or body or trustees.

III
MANAGEMENT AND ADMINISTRATION OF PROPERTY

7. Management of property by government

(1) Notwithstanding anything contained in any contract or instrument or order of any court, tribunal or other authority to the contrary, on and from the commencement of this Act, the property vested in the Central Government under Section 3 shall be managed by the Central Government or by a person or body of persons or trustees of any trust authorised by that government in this behalf.

(2) In managing the property vested in the Central Government under Section 3, the Central

Government or the authorised person shall ensure that the position existing before the commencement of this Act in the area on which the structure (including the premises of the inner and outer courtyards of such structure), commonly known as Ramjanmabhoomi-Babri Masjid, stood in Village Kot Ramachandra in Ayodhya, in Pargana Haveli, Avadh, in *teshil* Faizabad Sadar, in the district of Faizabad of the state of Uttar Pradesh is maintained.

IV
MISCELLANEOUS

8. Payment of amount

(1) The owner of any land, building, structure or other property comprised in the area shall be given by the Central Government, for the transfer to and vesting in that government under Section 3 of that land, building, structure or other property, in cash an amount equivalent to the market value of the land, building, structure or other property.

(2) The Central Government shall, for the purpose of deciding the claim of the owner or any person having a claim against the owner under sub-section (1), by notification in the Official Gazette, appoint a Claims Commissioner.

(3) The Claims Commissioner shall regulate his own procedure for receiving and deciding the claims.

(4) The owner or any person having a claim against the owner may make a claim to the Claims Commissioner within a period of ninety days from the date of commencement of this Act:

PROVIDED that if the Claims Commissioner is satisfied that the claimant was prevented by sufficient cause from preferring the claim within the said period of ninety days, the Claims Commissioner may entertain the claim within a further period of ninety days and not thereafter.

9. Act to override all other enactments

The provisions of this Act shall have effect notwithstanding anything inconsistent therewith contained in any other law for the time being in force or any instrument having effect by virtue of any law other than this Act or any decree or order of any court, tribunal or other authority.

10. Penalties

Any person who is in charge of the management of the area and fails to deliver to the Central Government or the authorised person any asset, register or other document in his custody relating to such area or, as the case may be, authenticated copies of such register or document, shall be punishable with imprisonment for a term which may extend to three years or with fine which may extend to ten thousand rupees, or with both.

11. Protection of action taken in good faith

No suit, prosecution or other legal proceeding shall lie against the Central Government or the authorised person or any of the officers or other employees of that government or the authorised person for anything which is in good faith done or intended to be done under this Act.

12. Power to make rules

(1) The Central Government may, by notification in the Official Gazette, make rules to carry out the provisions of this Act.

(2) Every rule made by the Central Government under this Act shall be laid, as soon as may be after it is made, before each House of Parliament,

while it is in session, for a total period of thirty days which may be comprised in one session or in two or more successive sessions, and if, before the expiry of the session immediately following the session or the successive sessions aforesaid, both Houses agree in making any modification in the rule or both Houses agree that the rule should not be made, the rule shall thereafter have effect only in such modified form or be of no effect, as the case may be; so, however, that any such modification or annulment shall be without prejudice to the validity of anything previously done under that rule.

13. Repeal and saving

(1) Subject to the provisions of sub-section (2), the Acquisition of Certain Area at Ayodhya Ordinance, 1993 (Ord. 8 of 1993), is hereby repealed.

(2) Notwithstanding anything contained in the said ordinance,

(a) the right, title and interest in relation to plot No. 242 situated in Village Kot Ramachandra specified against Sl. No. 1 of the Schedule to the said ordinance shall be deemed never to have been transferred to, and vested in, the Central Government;

(b) any suit, appeal or other proceeding in respect of the right, title and interest relating to the said plot No. 242, pending before any court, tribunal or other authority, shall be deemed never to have abated and such suit, appeal or other proceeding (including the orders or interim orders of any court thereon) shall be deemed to have been restored to the position existing immediately before the commencement of the said ordinance;

(c) any other action taken or thing done under that ordinance in relation to the said plot No. 242 shall be deemed never to have been taken or done.

(3) Notwithstanding such repeal, anything done or any action taken under the said ordinance shall be deemed to have been done or taken under the corresponding provisions of this Act.

The Schedule
[See Section 2(a)]
Description of the Area

The Central Government's move to acquire the land was challenged in court. The Supreme Court in 1994 upheld the acquisition laid out in 'The Acquisition of Certain Area at Ayodhya Act, 1993', while holding a few of its provisions as unconstitutional. The key findings are given below:

M. Ismail Faruqui (Dr) v. Union of India, (1994) 6 SCC 360

Bench: Chief Justice M.N. Venkatachalliah, Justice A.M. Ahmadi, Justice J.S. Verma, Justice G.N. Ray and Justice S.P. Bharucha.

Key excerpts from the judgement (*Ayodhya's Rama Temple in Courts* by Virag Gupta):

It may also be mentioned that even as Ayodhya is said to be of particular significance to the Hindus as a place of pilgrimage because of the ancient belief that Lord Rama was born there, the mosque was of significance for the Muslim community as an ancient mosque built by Mir Baqi in 1528 A.D. As a mosque, it was a religious place of worship by the Muslims. This indicates the comparative significance of the disputed site to the two communities and also that the impact of acquisition is equally on the right and interest of the Hindu community. Mention of this aspect is made only in the context of the argument that the statute as a whole, not merely Section 7 thereof, is anti-secular being slanted in favour of the Hindus and against the Muslims.

Section 7(2) of the Act freezes the situation admittedly in existence on 7-1-1993 which was a lesser right of worship for the Hindu devotees than that in existence earlier for a long time till the demolition of the disputed structure on 6-12-1992; and it does not create a new situation more favourable to the Hindu community amounting to conferment on them of a larger right of worship in the disputed site than that practised till 6-12-1992. Maintenance of status quo as on 7-1-1993 does not, therefore, confer or have the effect of granting to the Hindu community any further benefit thereby. It is also pertinent to bear in mind that the persons responsible for demolition of the mosque on 6-12-1992 were some miscreants who cannot be identified and equated with the entire Hindu community and, therefore, the act of vandalism so perpetrated by the miscreants cannot be treated as an act of the entire Hindu community for the purpose of adjudging the constitutionality of the enactment. Strong reaction against, and condemnation by the Hindus of the demolition of the structure in general bears eloquent testimony to this fact. Rejection of Bharatiya Janata Party at the hustings in the subsequent elections in Uttar Pradesh is another circumstance to that effect. The miscreants who demolished the mosque had no religion, caste or creed except the character of a criminal and the mere incident of birth of such a person in any particular community cannot attach the stigma of his crime to the community in which he was born.

Another effect of the freeze imposed by Section 7(2) of the Act is that it ensures that there can be no occasion for the Hindu community to seek to enlarge the scope of the practice of worship by them as on 7-1-1993 during the interregnum till the final adjudication on the basis that in fact a larger right of worship by them was in vogue up to 6-12-1992. It is difficult to visualise how Section 7(2) can be construed as a slant in favour of the Hindu community and, therefore, anti-secular. The provision does not curtail practice of right of worship of the Muslim community in the disputed area, there having been de facto no exercise of the practice or worship by them there at least since December 1949; and it maintains status quo by the freeze to the reduced right of worship by the Hindus as in existence on 7-1-1993. However, confining exercise of the right of worship of the Hindu community to its reduced form within the disputed area as on 7-1-1993, lesser than that exercised till the demolition on 6-12-1992, by the freeze enacted in Section 7(2) appears to be reasonable and just in view of the fact that the miscreants who demolished the mosque are suspected to be persons professing to practise the Hindu religion. The Hindu community must, therefore, bear the cross on its chest, for the misdeed of the miscreants reasonably suspected to belong to their religious fold.

This is the proper perspective, we say, in which the statute as a whole and Section 7 in particular must be viewed. Thus the factual foundation for challenge to the statute as a whole and Section 7(2) in particular on the ground of secularism, a basic feature of the constitution, and the rights to equality and freedom of religion is non-existent.

Reference may be made to the statements of the Central Government soon after the demolition on 7-12-1992 and 27-12-1992 wherein it was said that the mosque would be rebuilt. It was urged that the action taken on 7-1-1993 to issue an ordinance, later replaced by the Act, and simultaneously to make the reference to this court under Article 143(1) of the constitution amounts to resiling from the earlier statements for the benefit of the Hindu community. It is sufficient to say that the earlier statements so made cannot limit the power of Parliament and are not material for adjudging the constitutional validity of the enactment. The validity of the statute has to be determined on the touchstone of the constitution and not any statements made prior to it. We have therefore no doubt that Section 7 does not suffer from the infirmity of being anti-secular or discriminatory to render it unconstitutional.

To appreciate the stand of the Central Government on this point, we permitted the learned Solicitor General to make a categorical statement for the Union of India in this behalf. The final statement made by the learned Solicitor General of India in writing dated 14-9-1994 forming a part of the record, almost at the conclusion of the hearing, also does not indicate that the answer to the question referred would itself be decisive of the core question in controversy between the parties to the suits relating to the claim over the disputed site. According to the statement, the Central Government proposes to resort to a process of negotiation between the rival claimants after getting the answer to the question referred, and if the negotiations fail, then to adopt such course as it may find appropriate in the circumstances. There can be no doubt, in these circumstances, that the special reference made under Article 143(1) of the constitution cannot be construed as an effective alternate dispute-resolution mechanism to permit substitution of the pending suits and legal proceedings by the mode adopted of making this reference. In our opinion, this fact alone is sufficient to invalidate sub-section (3) of Section 4 of the Act [*see* Indira Nehru Gandhi v. Raj Narain [1975 Supp SCC 1: (1976) 2 SCR 347]. We accordingly declare sub-section (3) of Section 4 to be unconstitutional. However, sub-section

(3) of Section 4 is severable, and, therefore, its invalidity is not an impediment to the remaining statute being upheld as valid.

As a result of the above discussion, our conclusions, to be read with the discussion, are as follows:

(1)(a) Sub-section (3) of Section 4 of the Act abates all pending suits and legal proceedings without providing for an alternative dispute-resolution mechanism for resolution of the dispute between the parties thereto. This is an extinction of the judicial remedy for resolution of the dispute amounting to negation of rule of law. Sub-section (3) of Section 4 of the Act is, therefore, unconstitutional and invalid.

(b) The remaining provisions of the Act do not suffer from any invalidity on the construction made thereof by us. Sub-section (3) of Section 4 of the Act is severable from the remaining Act. Accordingly, the challenge to the constitutional validity of the remaining Act, except for sub-section (3) of Section 4, is rejected.

(2) Irrespective of the status of a mosque under the Muslim Law applicable in the Islamic countries, the status of a mosque under the Mohammedan Law applicable in secular India is the same and equal to that of any other place of worship of any religion; and it does not enjoy any greater immunity from acquisition in exercise of the sovereign or prerogative power of the State, than that of the places of worship of the other religions.

(3) The pending suits and other proceedings relating to the disputed area within which the structure (including the premises of the inner and outer courtyards of such structure), commonly known as the Ramjanmabhoomi-Babri Masjid, stood, stand revived for adjudication of the dispute therein, together with the interim orders made, except to

the extent the interim orders stand modified by the provisions of Section 7 of the Act.

(4) The vesting of the said disputed area in the Central Government by virtue of Section 3 of the Act is limited, as a statutory receiver, with the duty for its management and administration according to Section 7 requiring maintenance of status quo therein under sub-section (2) of Section 7 of the Act. The duty of the Central Government as the statutory receiver is to hand over the disputed area in accordance with Section 6 of the Act, in terms of the adjudication made in the suits for implementation of the final decision therein. This is the purpose for which the disputed area has been so acquired.

(5) The power of the courts in making further interim orders in the suits is limited to, and circumscribed by, the area outside the ambit of Section 7 of the Act.

(6) The vesting of the adjacent area, other than the disputed area, acquired by the Act in the Central Government by virtue of Section 3 of the Act is absolute with the power of management and administration thereof in accordance with sub-section (1) of Section 7 of the Act, till its further vesting in any authority or other body or trustees of any trust in accordance with Section 6 of the Act. The further vesting of the adjacent area, other than the disputed area, in accordance with Section 6 of the Act has to be made at the time and in the manner indicated, in view of the purpose of its acquisition.

(7) The meaning of the word 'vest' in Section 3 and Section 6 of the Act has to be so understood in the different contexts.

(8) Section 8 of the Act is meant for payment of compensation to owners of the property vesting absolutely in the Central Government, the title to

which is not in dispute being in excess of the disputed area, which alone is the subject matter of the revived suits. It does not apply to the disputed area, title to which has to be adjudicated in the suits and in respect of which the Central Government is merely the statutory receiver as indicated, with the duty to restore it to the owner in terms of the adjudication made in the suits.

(9) The challenge to acquisition of any part of the adjacent area on the ground that it is unnecessary for achieving the professed objective of settling the long-standing dispute cannot be examined at this stage. However, the area found to be superfluous on the exact area needed for the purpose being determined on adjudication of the dispute, must be restored to the undisputed owners.

(10) Rejection of the challenge by the undisputed owners to acquisition of some religious properties in the vicinity of the disputed area, at this stage is with the liberty granted to them to renew their challenge, if necessary at a later appropriate stage, in case of continued retention by Central Government of their property in excess of the exact area determined to be needed on adjudication of the dispute.

Consequently, the Special Reference No. 1 of 1993 [Ed.: For Order dated January 27, 1993 of the present bench on the reference, *see* (1993) 1 SCC 642] made by the President of India under Article 143(1) of the Constitution of India is superfluous and unnecessary and does not require to be answered. For this reason, we very respectfully decline to answer it and return the same.

The questions relating to the constitutional validity of the said Act and maintainability of the Special Reference are decided in these terms.

□

9

Supreme Court Verdict on Ramjanmabhoomi

Initially, five lawsuits were filed in the lower court related to Ramjanmabhoomi. The first law suit was filed by Gopal Singh Visharad, a devotee of Ram Lalla, in 1950. Visharad sought enforcement of the right to worship of Hindus at the disputed site. In the same year, Paramahans Ramachandra Das had also filed the lawsuit for continuation of worship and keeping the idols under the central dome of the now-demolished disputed structure. But this plea was later withdrawn. In 1959, a Hindu group by the name of Nirmohi Akhara moved the trial court. It sought management and *shebaiti* (devotee) rights over the 2.77 acre disputed land. In 1961, Uttar Pradesh Sunni Central Waqf Board moved the court. It claimed title right over the disputed property. In 1989, the deity, 'Ram Lalla Virajman', moved the lawsuit, seeking title right over the entire disputed property through next friend (*sakha*) and former Allahabad High Court judge Deoki Nandan Agrawal. All these lawsuits were transferred to the Allahabad High Court for adjudication after demolition of the Babri structure on 6 December, 1992.

The judgement of the Allahabad High Court in Ramjanmabhhoomi case was delivered on 30 September, 2010. It ruled that the 2.77-acre land in Ayodhya, where both Hindus and Muslims laid their claim and hence it became the 'disputed land', to be partitioned equally among the three parties -- the

Sunni Waqf Board, the Nirmohi Akhara and Ram Lalla.

Fourteen appeals were filed in the Supreme Court against this judgement. Since 2011, the matter was pending without a final verdict before the apex court during the tenure of following Chief Justices of India:

(i) Hon'ble Mr. Justice S.H. Kapadia 2. Hon'ble Mr. Justice Altamas Kabir 3. Hon'ble Mr. Justice P. Sathasivam 4. Hon'ble Mr. Justice R.M. Lodha 5. Hon'ble Mr. Justice H.L. Dattu 6. Hon'ble Mr. Justice T.S. Thakur 7. Hon'ble Mr. Justice J.S. Khehar 8. Hon'ble Mr. Justice Dipak Misra.

A five-judge bench headed by Chief Justice of India, Hon'ble Mr. Justice Ranjan Gogoi delivered the much-awaited final verdict on 9 November, 2019. The four other judges on this bench were Hon'ble Justices S.A. Bobde, Ashok Bhushan, D.Y. Chandrachud and S. Abdul Nazeer.

Eighteen review petitions were filed in the Supreme Court for further review on the Ayodhya land dispute case after the above-mentioned verdict. A five-judge bench rejected all these petitions on 12 December, 2019.

The in-chamber proceedings on these petitions were held as taken up by a bench headed by Chief Justice S.A. Bobde and also comprising Justices D.Y. Chandrachud, Ashok Bhushan, S.A. Nazeer and Sanjeev Khanna.

Justice Khanna was not a part of the five-judge constitution bench that had delivered the earlier verdict. He had replaced the then Chief Justice of India Ranjan Gogoi, who had retired on 17 November, 2019.

Following are the key highlights of the Ayodhya verdict delivered on 9 November, 2019:

- The possession of disputed land to be handed over to the deity Ram Lalla, one of the three litigants in the case.

- Sunni Waqf Board to be allotted five acres of alternative land to build a new mosque.
- The Union Government should frame a scheme within three months and set up a trust for construction of a temple.

Here are some more key takeaways from the Supreme Court's judgement pronounced in Ramjanmabhoomi case:

- The bench pronounced a unanimous decision.
- There is an addendum to the judgement attached from pp. No. 930 to 1045 which incorporates reasoning of one of the Hon'ble Judges on whether the disputed structure is the birthplace of Lord Rama according to the faith and belief of the Hindu devotees. This set of reasoning is more prominent in favour of the Hindus.
- At the beginning of the pronouncement, the court dismissed the SLP filed by Shia Waqf Board on the ground of unexplained inordinate delay.
- The court dismissed the suit filed by Nirmohi Akhara.
- The court said: "The Central Government shall, within a period of three months from the date of this judgement, formulate a scheme pursuant to the powers vested in it under Sections 6 and 7 of the Acquisition of Certain Area of Ayodhya Act, 1993. The scheme shall envisage the setting up of a trust with a Board of Trustees or any other appropriate body under the section. The scheme to be framed by the Central Government shall make necessary provisions in regard to the functioning of the trust or body, including on matters relating to the management of the trust, the powers of the trustees, including the construction of a temple and all necessary incidental and supplemental matters;

"possession of the inner and outer courtyards shall be

handed over to the Board of Trustees of the trust or to the body so constituted. The Central Government will be at liberty to make suitable provisions in respect of the rest of the acquired land by handing it over to the trust or body for management and development in terms of the scheme framed in accordance with the above directions; and

"possession of the disputed property shall continue to vest in the statutory receiver under the Central Government, until in exercise of its jurisdiction under Section 6 of the Ayodhya Act of 1993, a notification is issued vesting the property in the trust or other body.

"Simultaneously, with the handing over of the disputed property to the trust or body...a suitable plot of land measuring 5 acres shall be handed over to the Sunni Central Waqf Board.

(ii) The land shall be allotted either by:

(a) the Central Government out of the land acquired under the Ayodhya Act 1993; or

(b) the state government at a suitable prominent place in Ayodhya.

"The Central Government and the state government shall act in consultation with each other to effectuate the above allotment in the period stipulated.

"The Sunni Central Waqf Board would be at liberty, on the allotment of the land, to take all necessary steps for the construction of a mosque on the land so allotted together with other associated facilities. The directions for the allotment of land to the Sunni Central Waqf Board... are issued in pursuance of the powers vested in this court under Article 142 of the constitution."

The court further added, "In exercise of the powers vested in this court under Article 142 of the constitution, we direct that in the scheme to be framed by the Central Government, appropriate representation may be given in the trust or body, to the Nirmohi Akhara in such manner as the Central

Government deems fit.

"To sum it up, the disputed land/the area under the mosque has been given to the Plaintiff No. 1 in Suit No. 5. Possession of inner and outer courtyards shall be directed to be handed over to the Board of Trustees formulated under the scheme of Sections 6 and 7 of the Ayodhya Act, 1993. The trust so formed under the scheme may have appropriate representation from Nirmohi Akhara as the Central Government deems fit.

"Simultaneously, when disputed property will be given to the trust, a suitable plot of 5 acres shall be handed over to Sunni Waqf Board. This 5 acre land shall be either from the acquired land by the Act of 1993 or it will be provided by the state government at a prominent place in Ayodhya. This direction has been issued under Article 142 of the Constitution."

Issue-wise Reasoning

Part C: This part of the judgement deals with the volumes of the evidence and finally takes note of the exact dispute and admission on part of Muslims that Lord Rama was born in Ayodhya.

"Para 45...There is, in other words, no dispute before this court in regard to the faith and belief of the Hindus that the birth of Lord Rama is ascribed to have taken place at Ayodhya, as described in Valmiki's *Ramayana*. What is being disputed is whether the disputed site below the central dome of the Babri Masjid is the place of birth of Lord Rama. The Muslim parties have expressly denied the existence of a Ramjanmabhoomi temple at the site of Babri Masjid. With this background, it becomes necessary to advert to the salient aspects of the documentary evidence which has emerged on the record."

Part F of the judgement from pp. 82 to 84 enlists points for determination in the present set of appeals.

Part G of the judgement deals with the authenticity and the value of three inscriptions obtained from the site to decide the time of construction and the person who has constructed the structure.

The court has concluded in Para 68 that, "... the precise date of the construction of the mosque is a matter which has no practical relevance to the outcome of the controversy having regard to the pleadings in Suits 4 and 5 and the positions adopted by the contesting Hindu and Muslim parties before this court."

Part H: The court has given its reasoning on judicial review and characteristic of a mosque in Islamic law from pp. 114 to 115 of the judgement and rejected the contentions raised by the Hindu parties.

"Para 77... it is inappropriate for this court to enter upon an area of theology and to assume the role of an interpreter of the Hadees. The true test is whether those who believe and worship have faith in the religious efficacy of the place where they pray. The belief and faith of the worshipper in offering *namaz* at a place, which is for the worshipper a mosque, cannot be challenged. It would be preposterous for this court to question it on the ground that a true Muslim would not offer prayer in a place which does not meet an extreme interpretation of doctrine selectively advanced by Mr Mishra. This court, as a secular institution, set up under a constitutional regime, must steer clear from choosing one among many possible interpretations of theological doctrine and must defer to the safer course of accepting the faith and belief of the worshipper.

"Above all, the practice of religion, Islam being no exception, varies according to the culture and social context. That indeed is the strength of our plural society.

"Cultural assimilation is a significant factor which shapes the manner in which religion is practiced. In the plural diversity of religious beliefs as they are practiced in India, cultural assimilation cannot be construed as a feature destructive of religious doctrine. On the contrary, this process strengthens and reinforces the true character of a country which has been able to preserve its unity by accommodating, tolerating and respecting a diversity of religious faiths and ideas.

"... For the devotees of Lord Rama... Bhagwan Sri Rama Virajman is the embodiment of Lord Rama and constitutes the resident deity of Ramjanmabhoomi. The faith and belief of the Hindu devotees is a matter personal to their conscience and it is not for this court to scrutinise the strength of their convictions or the rationality of their beliefs beyond a prima facie examination to ascertain whether such beliefs are held in good faith.

"The oral and documentary evidence shows that the Hindu devotees of Lord Rama hold a genuine, long-standing and profound belief in the religious merit attained by offering prayer to Lord Rama at the site they believe to be his birthplace. Evidence has been led to show a long practice of Hindu worship to Lord Rama at the disputed site. The travel logs of Joseph Tieffenthaler in the eighteenth century and Robert Montgomery Martin in the early nineteenth century record the prevalence of Hindu worship at the disputed site.

"They also refer to special occasions such as Ramnavmi during which Hindu devotees converged upon the *janmasthan* from distant areas motivated by the desire to offer prayer to Lord Rama. The continued faith and belief of the Hindu devotees in the existence of the *janmasthan* below the three-domed structure is evidenced by the activities of the Nirmohis, individual devotees such as Nihang Sikhs and the endless stream of Hindu devotees over the years who visited the disputed site. This is testament to the long-held belief in the sanctity of the disputed site as a place of worship for the Hindu religion.

"For the present purposes, it is sufficient to note that the factum of Hindu belief in the sanctity of the disputed site is established by evidence."

On Legal Personality of Plaintiff No. 1 in Suit No. 5: Recognised.

The court said, "It is true that the connection between a person and what they consider divine is deeply internal. It lies in the realm of a personal sphere in which no other person must intrude. It is for this reason that the constitution protects the freedom to profess, practice and propagate religion equally to all citizens. Often, the human condition finds solace in worship. But worship may not be confined into a straightjacket formula. It is on the basis of the deep entrenchment of religion into the social fabric of Indian society that the right to religious freedom was not made absolute. An attempt has been made in the jurisprudence of this court to demarcate the religious from the secular. The adjudication of civil claims over private property must remain within the domain of the secular if the commitment to constitutional values is to be upheld. Over four decades ago, the constitution was amended and a specific reference to its secular fabric was incorporated in the Preamble. At its heart, this reiterated what the constitution always respected and accepted: the equality of all faiths. Secularism cannot be a writ lost in the sands of time by being oblivious to the exercise of religious freedom by everyone.

"The Hindus continued to worship at the *Ramchabutra* which was in the outer courtyard; there can be no manner of doubt that this was in furtherance of their belief that the birthplace of Lord Rama was within the precincts of and under the central dome of the mosque.

"The Muslim account of worship prior to 1856 is conspicuously silent as opposed to the accounts of worship being offered by the Hindu. Though the claim of the Muslims over the inner courtyard was not abandoned, yet as the evidence indicates, this was a matter of contestation and dispute (para 787)."

Archaeological report discussed at page 598:

The ASI report does find the existence of a pre-existing structure. The report concludes on the basis of the architectural fragments found at the site and the nature of the structure that it was of a Hindu religious origin (para 511). Then finally the court has held that "the Hindus have established a clear case of a possessory title to the outside courtyard by virtue of long, continued and unimpeded worship at the *Ramchabutra* and other objects of religious significance.

"The Hindus and the Muslims have contested claims to the offering worship within the three-domed structure in the inner courtyard. The assertion by the Hindus of their entitlement to offer worship inside has been contested by the Muslims."

Moulding of relief by the HC

"From Para 789 to 794 (starting from p. No. 915) of the judgement the court has held the approach taken by the HC to trifurcate the land was erroneous. When the suit was not of partition and upon barring the suit by limitation, granting the relief through trifurcation was held not sustainable.

"**Para 791:** In assessing the correctness of the decree of the High Court, it must be noted at the outset that the High Court was not seized of a suit for partition. In a suit for partition, it is trite law that every party is both a plaintiff and defendant.

"The High Court was called upon to decide the question of title particularly in the declaratory suits, Suits 4 and 5.

"It granted reliefs which were not the subject matter of the prayers in the suits. In the process of doing so, it proceeded to assume the jurisdiction of a civil court in a suit for partition, which the suits before it were not.

"**Para 792:** ...This provision does not entitle the court in a civil trial to embark upon the exercise of recasting virtually the frame of a suit, which was undertaken by the High Court. There was no basis in the pleadings before the High Court and certainly no warrant in the reliefs which were claimed to direct a division of the land in the manner that a court would do in a suit for partition.

"**Para 794:** There is another serious flaw in the entire approach of the High Court in granting relief of a three-way bifurcation of the disputed site. Having come to the conclusion that Suit 3 (filed by Nirmohi Akhara) and Suit 4 (filed by Sunni Central Waqf Board) were barred by limitation, the High Court proceeded to grant relief in Suit 5 to the plaintiffs in Suits 3 and 4. This defies logic and is contrary to settled principles of law. Moreover, the claim by the Nirmohi Akhara was as a *shebait* who claimed a decree for management and charge. On its own case, Nirmohi Akhara could not have been granted an independent share of the land.

"**Para 797:** As regard to the outer courtyard, the court has held that there is clear evidence that Hindus performed worship in outer courtyard unimpeded and the possession with regard to it is established completely.

"**Para 798:** As regard to the inner courtyard, worship by Hindus prior to the annexation of Avadh by the British in 1857, is proved on balancing the evidence on preponderance of probabilities against the Muslims, who have offered no evidence to indicate that they were in exclusive possession of the inner structure prior to 1857 since the date of the construction is 1528. After 1857, there is evidence to indicate that *namaz* has been offered within its premise and also last Friday *namaz* was offered on 16th December, 1949.

"**Para 799:** Three-way bifurcation by the High Court was wrong and will not sub-serve the interest of parties or to secure a lasting sense of peace and tranquillity.

"**Para 800:** First plaintiff (Ram Lalla Virajman) has been held as juristic person and next friend entitled to represent him... Allotment of alternate land to Muslims is necessary because the evidence in respect of possessory claim of the Hindus to the composite whole of the disputed property stands on a better footing than the evidence adduced by the Muslims, as the Muslims were dispossessed first on 22nd/23rd December, 1949 which was ultimately destroyed on 6th December, 1992. Court has exercised its power under Article 142 to remedy this wrong committed against Muslims."

□

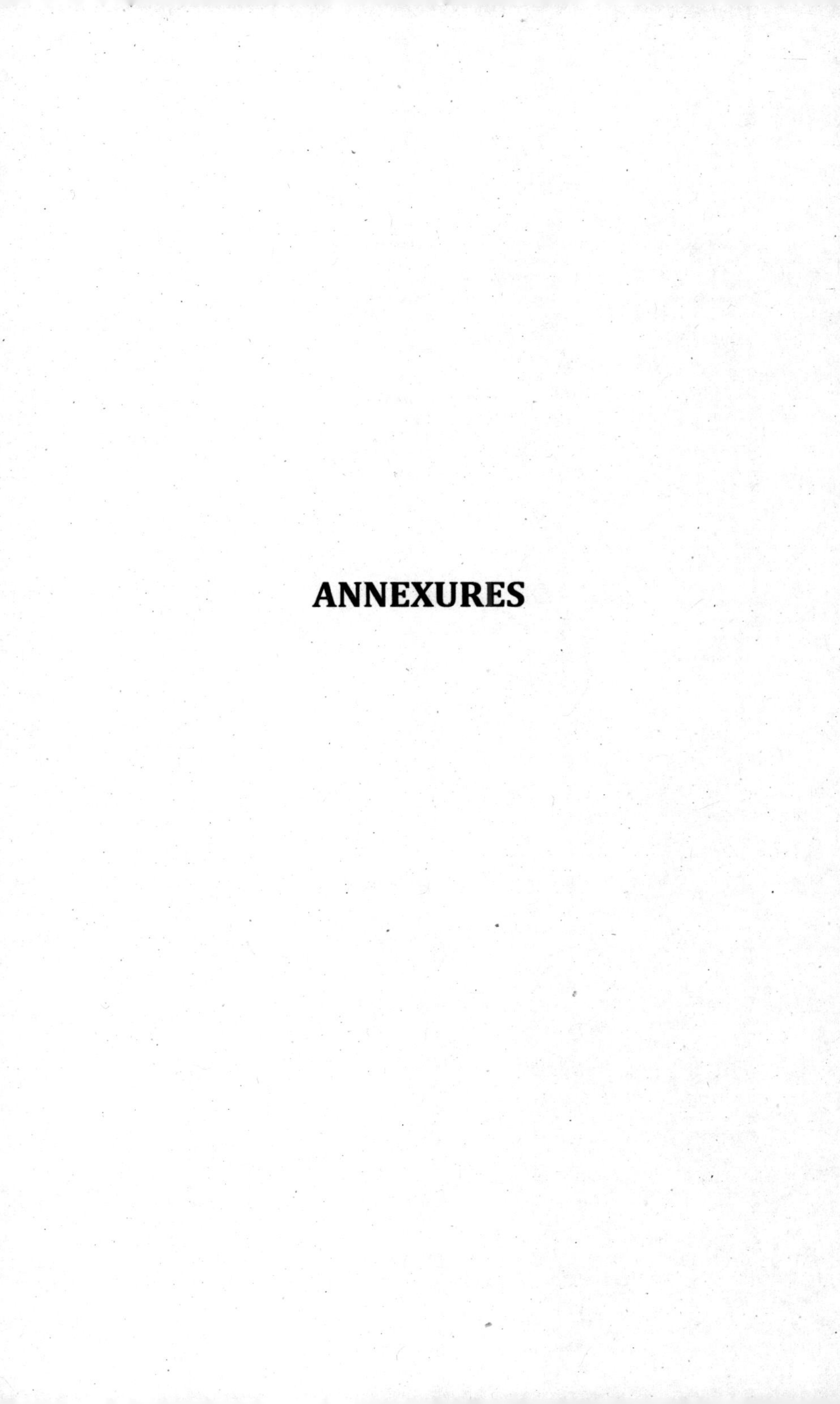

ANNEXURES

Annexure 1

Chronology of legal issues post-independence

1949: On the night of 22.12.1949, the idol of Bhagwan Shri Rama was installed after performing the ceremony of *pran pratishtha* under the central dome of the building.

23.12.1949: Thereafter an FIR was lodged that some persons trespassed into the inner courtyard and placed idols of Lord Rama.

29.12.1949: On 29.12.1949, City Magistrate passed an order under Section 145 Cr.P.C. calling upon the Muslims and Hindus. He also ordered attachment of entire premises as the case being one of the emergency and directed the attached property in the charge of Sri Priya Dutt Ram.

5.1.1950: The receiver took charge of the premises on 05.01.1950 and inventory was prepared and all the movable properties were attached.

16.1.1950: The first suit being Civil Suit No. 1 of 1950 was filed on 16.01.1950 for declaration and injunction by Gopal Singh Visharad in the court of Civil Judge, Faizabad along with an application under O39 R2 and Sec. 151 CPC and on the same day an interim injunction as prayed was granted.

19.01.1950: In Suit 1 of 1950, after service of summons all

the parties appeared and court modified the injunction dated 16.1.1950 in the following manner:

"Opposite parties are hereby restrained by means of temporary injunction to refrain from removing the idols in question from the site in dispute and from interfering with pooja, *etc. as at present carried on."*

Affidavits were filed by Muslims who were residents of Ayodhya before the Magistrate in proceedings under Section 145 Cr.P.C. wherein they admitted that since 1934, Muslims have not offered any *namaz* in the disputed building and it is continuously in possession of the Hindus and also they have no objection in case the disputed building is handed over to Hindus.

5.12.1950: Suit No. 25 of 1950 (later on numbered as OOS 2 of 1989) was filed by Paramhans Ramachandra Das seeking an injunction restraining the defendants from interfering with the worship of Lord Rama at the place Janmabhoomi and further not to disturb or remove the idols kept on that date.

01.02.1951: By order of Civil Judge, Faizabad, Suit No. 25 of 1950 was consolidated with Suit No.1 of 1950.

03.03.1951: The objections to the ex parte injunction dated 16.1.1950 (modified on 19.1.1950) passed in Suit No.1 were considered and the interim injunction was confirmed.

26.04.1955: Appeal preferred against the order of injunction was also dismissed by the High Court.

17.12.1959: Nirmohi Akhara filed original Suit No. 26 of 1959 (OOS 3 of 1989) (Suit 3) for removal from management and charge of temple Janmabhoomi and delivery of the same.

18.12.1961: Suit No.4 was filed by Sunni Central Board of Waqf being R.S. No. 120 of 1961 and application under Order 1 Rule 8 was also filed alongwith it.

06.01.1964: Joint applications were filed on behalf of all the parties in Suits 1, 2 3 and 4 requesting for consolidation of all the suits and the same was allowed with the consent of all the parties and Suit-4, Sunni Central Waqf Board v. Gopal Singh was ordered to be the leading case.

17.07.1965: Additional issue was framed:
"Whether valid notification u/s 5(1) of U.P. Muslim Waqf Act of 1936 relating to the property was ever done? If so, its effect."

Issue no. 17 was taken up as primary preliminary issue.

21.04.1966: Vide judgement dated 21.4.1966, Civil Judge decided the same against plaintiffs (Suit-4) and in favour of defendants therein. It is observed that:
"... After perusing the alleged notification dated 26.2.1944 said to have been published under Section 5 of 1936 Act, the court found that Item 26, at which the alleged Waqf of Waqif Badshah Babur was mentioned, was blank in its last column and consequently it did not give any idea of the property of which Waqf was created. It held that the alleged government notification at Item No. 26 was meaningless ..."

Jan. 1986: An application was filed in January, 1986 before Munsif Sadar, Faizabad by one Sri Umesh Chandra Pandey, advocate in Suit 1, stating that the authorities are violating injunction order by not permitting unobstructed worship.

25.1.1986: Another application was filed by Sri Umesh Chandra Pandey, advocate seeking a direction to defendants No. 6 to 9 (Suit-1) not to create any obstruction in *darshan, pooja,* etc. by keeping the premises under lock and key.

Ld. Munsif deferred the matter observing that the original record of the leading suit had already been summoned by the High Court and in the absence thereof, it is not proper to pass any order on the said application.

1.2.1986: Thereafter a revision was filed before the District Judge, Faizabad who treated the same as Misc. Appeal and passed Order dated 01.02.1986 directing to open the locks placed on the gate of the inner courtyard.

15.12.1987: The state government on 15.12.1987 moved an application No. 29 of 1987 under Section 24 read with 151 C.P.C. requesting High Court to withdraw all the suits pending in the court below at Faizabad for trial and disposal by High Court.

1.7.1989: Suit-5 was filed as a fresh suit on 1.7.1989 in the court of Civil Judge, Faizabad.

The reliefs sought in the suit are:

(a) a declaration that the entire premises of Shri Ramjanmabhoomi at Ayodhya, as described by Annexures I, II and III belong to plaintiff deities and

(b) a permanent injunction against the defendants prohibiting them from interfering with or raising any objection to, or placing any obstruction in the construction of the new temple building at Shri Ramjanmabhoomi, Ayodhya.

10.07.1989: All the cases were withdrawn and transferred to the High Court.

21.7.1989: On 21.07.1989, the Hon'ble Chief Justice constituted a Special Bench consisting of three judges.

07.10.1990: State of U.P. acquired 2.77 acres of land under Land Acquisition Act.

10.10.1991: Notification was issued under Section 6 of the Land Acquisition Act, 1894 and the purpose of acquisition as disclosed in the notification was "development of tourism and providing amenities to pilgrims at Ayodhya, District Faizabad."

16.10.1991: On 16.10.1991, writ petition No. 3540 of 1991 (M/B) was filed by Mohd. Hashim assailing the aforesaid notification, which was placed before the Special Bench.

11.12.1992: The aforesaid writ petitions were decided vide judgement dated 11.12.1992 and High Court struck down the aforesaid notification of acquisition of land measuring 2.7744 acres.

6.12.1992 and 7.12.1992:

On 06.12.1992 the disputed structure namely, temple Ramjanmabhoomi/Babri Masjid was demolished and on 07.12.1992 a temporary structure was created where the worship and *pooja* of Lord Rama/Ram Lalla and other deities was continued by the Hindus.

1.1.1993: WP No.110/1992 Vishwa Hindu Adhivakta Sangh vs. UOI along with WPs of Akhil Bhartiya Nehru Brigade, U.P. and Maharshi Avadesh:

Petition was allowed to the extent that opposite parties were commanded to allow Hindus and devotees *darshan* in a meaningful manner.

3.4.1993: The Central Government enacted Acquisition of Certain Area of Ayodhya Act, 1993 (Act No. 33 of 1993) (Ayodhya Act).

The Ayodhya Act was published in the *Gazette* dated 3rd April, 1993 and it came into force w.e.f. 7th January, 1993.

The total area sought to be acquired was 67.703 acres of land.

As a result of the said enactment, all the four suits, by operation of law, stood abated under Section 4(3) of the Act.

7.1.1993: The President of India also made a special reference to the Apex Court under Article 143(1) of the Constitution of India on the following question:

"Whether a Hindu temple or any Hindu religious structure existed prior to the construction of the Ramjanmabhoomi-Babri Masjid (including the premises of the inner and outer courtyards of such structure) in the area on which the structure stood?"

24.10.1994: The vires of Ayodhya Act was assailed before the High Court as well as before the Apex Court.

The Apex Court got the petitions filed before High Court transferred, heard all the matters collectively along with the reference made under Article 143 (1) of the constitution and decided vide its judgement dated 24.10.1994, reported as 1994 (6) SCC 360. The conclusion para is extracted hereunder:

"96. As a result of the above discussion, our conclusions, to be read with the discussion, are as follows:

(1)(a) sub-section (3) of Section 4 of the Act abates all pending suits and legal proceedings without providing for an alternative dispute-resolution mechanism for resolution of the dispute between the parties thereto. This is an

extinction of the judicial remedy for resolution of the dispute amounting to negation of rule of law. Sub-section (3) of Section 4 of the Act is, therefore, unconstitutional and invalid.

(b) The remaining provisions of the Act do not suffer from any invalidity on the construction made thereof by us. Sub-section (3) of Section 4 of the Act is severable from the remaining Act. Accordingly, the challenge to the constitutional validity of the remaining Act, except for sub-section (3) of Section 4, is rejected.

(2) Irrespective of the status of a mosque under the Muslim Law applicable in the Islamic countries, the status of a mosque under the Mohammedan Law applicable in secular India is the same and equal to that of any other place of worship of any religion; and it does not enjoy any greater immunity from acquisition in exercise of the sovereign or prerogative power of the State, than that of the places of worship of the other religions.

(3) The pending suits and other proceedings relating to the disputed area within which the structure (including the premises of the inner and outer courtyards of such structure), commonly known as the Ramjanmabhoomi-Babri Masjid, stood, stand revived for adjudication of the dispute therein, together with the interim orders made, except to the extent the interim orders stand modified by the provisions of Section 7 of the Act.

(4) The vesting of the said disputed area in the Central Government by virtue of Section 3 of the Act is limited, as a statutory receiver, with the duty for its management and administration according to Section 7 requiring maintenance of status quo

therein under sub-section (2) of Section 7 of the Act. The duty of the Central Government as the statutory receiver is to hand over the disputed area in accordance with Section 6 of the Act, in terms of the adjudication made in the suits for implementation of the final decision therein."

8.5.1996: Order dated 08.05.1996, noticing that there was no issue between the parties about the fact that Lord Rama is cultural heritage of India, and the citizens of country have a right to pay homage to his birthplace and in this admitted factual state of affairs, issue No. 14 as proposed at that time, was rejected.

24.7.1996: The recording of oral evidence commenced on 24.07.1996.

01.08.2002: The High Court noticed that the basic issue engaging attention of the Court in these suits is "whether there was a Hindu temple or any Hindu religious structure existed or the alleged Babri Masjid was constructed after demolishing the temple at the site in dispute."

High Court directed the parties to give their views/ suggestions, why the disputed land be not allowed to be excavated by Archaeological Survey of India.

High Court also directed ASI to get the disputed site surveyed by Ground Penetrating Radar or Geo-Radiology (GPR) and obtain report.

Sri Jilani, learned counsel for plaintiffs in Suit-4 in fact made a statement before the court that he has no objection on G.P.R. survey of the disputed site.

23.10.2002: All the objections raised by the parties were dealt and disposed of by the court vide Order dated 23.10.2002 and order for GPR/Geo-Radiology test was passed.

17.2.2002: The survey report was submitted by M/s Tozo through ASI.

05.03.2003: The said report was considered by the court after permitting parties to file their objections and the same were disposed of by order dated 5.3.2003 directing ASI to go ahead with the excavation of the disputed site.

22.08.2003: ASI submitted final report on 22.8.2003.

22.4.2009: Mr. Zafaryab Zilani, Mr. Mustaq Ahmad Siddiqui and Mr. Syed Irfan Ahmad, counsel for Muslim parties made statements UNDER ORDER X RULE 2 C.P.C. to the following effect:

"For the purpose of this case there is no dispute about the faith of Hindu devotees of Lord Rama regarding the birth of Lord Rama at Ayodhya as described in Balmiki Ramayana *or as existing today. It is, however, disputed and denied that the site of Babri Masjid was the place of birth of Lord Rama. It is also denied that there was any Ramjanmabhoomi temple at the site of Babri Masjid at any time whatsoever."*

30.9.2010: After hearing the parties at length, the Special Bench of Allahabad High Court delivered its judgement.

2010-2011: Appeals were preferred before Hon'ble Supreme Court, challenging the judgement of the High Court.

16.10.2019: Supreme Court concluded its proceedings in all the appeals after an elaborate hearing which continued on daily basis from 6.8.2019.

09.11.2019: Five-judge bench of Supreme Court headed by Chief Justice of India, Hon'ble Justice Ranjan Gogoi, delivered the verdict.

□

Annexure 2

Shri Ramjanmabhoomi Movement at a Glance

1. Ayodhya founded by Vaivasvata Manu (the progenitor and presiding figure of the current Manvantara, which is the 7th of the 14 that make up the current *kalpa*, each *kalpa* making up a day of Brahma) on the banks of the holy Saryu. He saved life on earth from the great deluge with the blessings and help of Bhagwan Matsyavatar. Two of his children, Ila and Ikshvaku became the progenitors of the lunar dynasty and solar dynasty respectively. The *saptarshis* (seven sages) in the Ministry of Vaivasvata Manu are Kashyapa, Atri, Vashishtha, Vishvamitra, Gautama, Jamadagni and Bharadvaja.
2. Birth of Lord Sri Rama, an incarnation of Bhagwan Vishnu, in the solar dynasty in Ayodhya lakhs of years ago in the Treta Yuga—the second of the four *yugas*, or ages of mankind—to rescue the world from global terrorism, wickedness and sensuousness and leave it happy, healthy and blessed for future generations.
3. Grand temple on 84 black touchstone pillars constructed by Sakari Samrat Vikramaditya 2100 years ago at Shri Ramjanmabhoomi (birthplace of Sri Rama), Ayodhya dedicated to Sri Rama to glorify

and perpetuate the memory of Sri Rama as a national and global hero and saviour. The birthplace was marked by temples of different ages as when the old ones got ruined by vagaries of nature including the Saryu floods, new ones came up to mark the site. According to experts, the pre-Babri temple was from the Ghadwal period.

4. Demolition of the said temple by Mir Baqi, Commander of the Muslim invader Babur in the year 1528 Common Era (CE) – 482 years ago.
5. First battle by Sri Rama *bhaktas* for 15 days to save the temple from Islamic marauders.
   The invaders could not overrun the temple and blast it by canons before 176,000 lionhearted Rama devotees had sacrificed their lives to save their most celebrated temple.
6. A *masjid*-like structure was forcefully superimposed on the demolished temple site, reusing the wreckage and remains of the temple, but the invaders could never construct the minarets for *azan* (call for prayer) and the mandatory water pool for *wazu*.
7. During the period from 1528 CE to 1949 CE there were 76 battles/struggles to reclaim the Ramjanmabhoomi site to reconstruct the temple. Guru Govind Singhji Maharaj, Maharani Raj Kunwar and many other greats fought to reclaim the holy place.
8. At midnight on 22nd December, 1949, Sri Ram Lalla (infant Sri Rama) revealed himself at the birthplace that was under the central dome of the structure. At that time Pt. Jawahar Lal Nehru was the Prime Minister of Bharat, Pt. Govind Ballabh Pant was the Chief Minister of Uttar Pradesh and Sri K.K. Nayyar from Kerala was the District Magistrate of Faizabad.

9. To maintain law and order, the City Magistrate attached the structure u/s 145 Cr.PC, appointed Sri Priya Dutt Ram as a receiver and entrusted the site to his care and ordered to lock the gates, but allowed a priest to go inside the structure and perform regular worship and rituals twice a day. The devotees were allowed only up to the locked gate. The local people and *sadhus* started chanting "*Sri Ram, Jai Ram, Jai Jai Ram.*"
   (Victory to Sri Rama) 24X7 Akhand Naam Sankeertan in front of the locked gate.
10. A veteran Congress leader of western U.P., Sri Dau Dayal Khanna, gave a rousing call to the Hindu society in March 1983 at Muzaffarnagar (U.P.) in a Hindu conference to reclaim the Ayodhya, Mathura and Kashi sites. Sri Gulzari Lal Nanda – two times interim Prime Minister of India after demise of PM Nehru and PM Shastri – was also present on the dais.
11. The First Dharma Sansad (National Parliament of *sants* and *dharmacharyas* of various branches of the Himalayan tradition) organised by VHP at Vigyan Bhavan, New Delhi in April 1984 resolved to reclaim Ayodhya first and have a Jan Jagaran Yatra (public awakening marathon all over the country) for unlocking the gate of the Janmabhoomi.
12. VHP started Ram-Janaki Rath Yatra from Sitamarhi to Ayodhya to Lucknow to Delhi for mass awakening in October, 1984. The *yatra* had, however, to be withdrawn for a year due to unfortunate developments in the country that year.
13. *Rath Yatras* restarted in October 1985 for mass awakening and with a demand to open the locks.
14. The Hindu society was so charged and exercised by these *Rath Yatras* that the District Judge of Faizabad

ordered on 1st of February, 1986 to open the locks. Sri Veer Bahadur Singh of Congress was the Chief Minister of U.P. and late Sri Rajiv Gandhi was the Prime Minister at that time.

15. A sketch for the proposed temple was drawn by Sri Chandrakant Bhai Sompura—a well-known temple architect of Gujarat—whose grandfather Padma Shri P.O. Sompura modelled the present Somnath temple and the family modelled many other Nagar style temples. Sri C.B. Sompuraji also prepared a wooden model of the Shri Ramjanmabhoomi temple.

16. In January 1989, on the holy occasion of Kumbh Mela at Prayagraj, on the banks of the Triveni Sangam, again a *Dharma Sansad* was organised by VHP and in the auspicious and august presence of Deoraha Baba it was decided to hold the *Ramshila poojan* programme at every temple of the country. The first brick was consecrated at Sri Badrinath Dham.

17. About 275,000 consecrated bricks (*Ramshilas*) from Bharat and abroad reached Ayodhya safely by the end of October 1989. An estimated 60 million people participated in the programme.

18. On 9 November, 1989 the foundation stone was laid by an S.C. brother Sri Kameswar Chowpal of Bihar with due permission of the then government. Sri Narayan Dutt Tiwari was the CM of U.P. and late Sri Rajiv Gandhi was the Prime Minister.

19. On 24th June of 1990 a declaration was made by *sadhus* to start *karseva* (voluntary service) to start the temple construction from *Devotthani Ekadashi* (30th October, 1990).

20. A *jyoti* (light/fire) was ignited by *arani manthan* (creating fire through the process of friction of wood blocks) at Ayodhya. It was called Ramjyoti. The *jyoti*

reached every Hindu home across the country and all celebrated Deepawali with this *jyoti*.

21. On 30.10.90, thousands of Rama devotees entered Ayodhya, crossing so many hurdles put up by the then U.P. government headed by Sri Mulayam Singh and a saffron flag was hoisted atop the disputed structure.
22. CM of U.P., Mulayam Singh Yadav ordered opening of fire on *karsevaks* on 2.11.90 in which so many lost their lives including the Kothari brothers – Sri Ram Kothari and Sri Sharad Kothari from Kolkata.
23. Delhi witnessed the grandest ever rally at Boat Club on 4.4.91. CM Mulayam Singh resigned.
24. In September '92, Sri Rama *padukapujan* was organised in all villages in India and another call was given to *bhaktas* to reach Ayodhya on *Gita Jayanti* (6th December, 1992). Millions of people reached for *karseva* and the world knows the fate of the Babri structure.
25. A stone slab, approx. 5 ft in length and 2.25 ft in width, was found from the demolished walls of the Babri structure. The epigraphists deciphered it to be an inscription of 20 lines written in Sanskrit of 12th century CE. The first line starts with '*Om Namah Shivaya.*' The 15th, 17th and the 19th lines speak about the details of the grand temple and the king who built it. The 15th line clearly mentions that the temple was dedicated to Vishnu Hari who killed Dasanan (Ravan). About 250 Hindu artifacts were also found from the rubble, that are presently under the control of the court.
26. Makeshift temple with tarpaulins was erected by *karsevaks* on the same spot where Sri Ram Lalla was seated before demolition. Approximately 67 acres

of land was acquired by an ordinance by the then Central Government headed by Sri P.V. Narasimha Rao in the name of safeguarding Sri Ram Lalla. This ordinance was approved by the Parliament through an Act on 7 January, 1993.

27. A lawyer, Hari Shankar Jain approached the Lucknow bench of Allahabad High Court for grant of permission for the regular *sewa-puja* of Sri Ram Lalla by devotees. Permission was granted on 1.1.1993. Since then the non-stop *darshan-pooja* has been going on.

28. The then Mahamahim President of India, Dr. Shankar Dayal Sharma referred a question to the Supreme Court under Article 143-A of the Constitution of India. The question was "Whether a Hindu temple or any Hindu religious structure existed prior to the construction of the Ramjanmabhoomi-Babri Masjid in the area on which the structure stood?" Also the acquisition by the Central Government was challenged by one Sri Ismail Farooqui and a few others.

29. The Supreme Court heard all the above petitions and also the special presidential reference jointly for about 20 months and delivered its judgement on 24th October, 1994.

The Supreme Court said: "The Lucknow Bench of Allahabad High Court would decide the title of the disputed site and answer the special reference made by the President."

30. A three-judge (two Hindus and one Muslim) full bench started hearing the matters in 1995. Issues were reframed. Oral evidences began to be recorded.

31. To find out the direct answer to the presidential special reference, in August 2002, the said bench

ordered Ground Penetrating Radar Survey (GPRS) of the site which was conducted by the Tojo Vikas International with its expert from Canada. The expert mentioned in his report the existence of a huge structure extending over a large area underneath the demolished structure, scientifically proving thereby that the Babri structure was not built on virgin land as was claimed by Muslims in their civil suit filed in December 1961 before the Civil Judge of Faizabad. The expert also gave his opinion to verify the GPRS report through scientific excavation.

32. In 2003, the High Court ordered the Archaeological Survey of India to excavate the site scientifically and verify the GPRS report. The excavation was conducted in the presence of two observers appointed by the court (two Additional District Judges of Faizabad). The parties concerned, their counsels, their experts/ representatives were permitted to remain present during excavation. To maintain impartiality, it was ordered that 40 per cent of the labour would be Muslims. Minute-to-minute videography and still photography of excavation were done by the ASI. The excavation was eye-opening. So many walls, floors, two rows of pillar-bases at 50 equidistant places were found. A Shiva temple was also seen. The GPRS report and the ASI report are now part and parcel of the High Court records.

33. The civil procedure of the court of law in the matter is now over after an exercise of about 60 years (40 years in the District Court and 20 years in the High Court) and the final verdict is expected by the end of September, 2010. Although all evidence is in favour of the Hindu claim that the Babri structure was superimposed on the Shri Ramjanmabhoomi site

after demolishing the temple that marked the site, still nobody can predict about the judgement. It is obvious that the judgement will create unrest in one party and its followers in the populace. This party may challenge the High Court verdict in the Supreme Court. The Supreme Court, however, may or may not take notice of it. In any case, every Indian citizen knows the fate of the Supreme Court judgement in Shah Bano case. The ball, thus, may finally be in the court of the Parliament of India as we have always been demanding that the Parliament should pass a law and handover the Sri Ramajanmabhoomi to the Hindu society.

34. In the original Constitution of India, there are illustrations of factors of Bharatiya national certitude. The third illustration in the said volume is that of Lord Rama and comrades returning to Ayodhya, riding the aerial vehicle Pushpak *viman* after his victory in Lanka.

35. The double-storeyed proposed temple with 108 pillars in each storey will be 270 ft. long, 135 ft. wide and 125 ft. high and the temple ringed by a 10 ft. wide *parikrama marg* (circumambulation path). Wall thickness will be 6 ft and door frames will be made of white Makrana marble. Carving work has been done at five workshops [two at Ayodhya (U.P.), one at Makrana (Rajasthan) and three at Pindwara (Rajasthan)]. 60 per cent of carving work is complete till date.

36. *Sants* and *dharmacharyas* in their meeting held on 5 April, 2010 at Haridwar Kumbh Mela, 2010 declared to organise Hanuman Chalisa *paath* all over the country under the banner of Sri Hanumat Shakti Jagaran Samiti, from Tulsi Jayanti (16th August, 2010)

to *Akshay Navami* (16th Nov., 2010) and Sri Hanumat Shakti Jagaran Maha Yajna in every *prakhand* during the month from Devotthani Ekadasi (17th Nov., 2010) to Gita Jayanti (16th Dec., 2010). These *yagnas* will be organised at approx. 8,000 centres in Bharat (*Source:* Vishwa Hindu Parishad).

□

Annexure 3

आस्ट्रियाई पादरी फादर टाइफेनथेलर की डायरी एवम् ब्रिटिश गजेटियरों में श्रीराम जन्मभूमि एवम् उस पर बाबर के आक्रमण का वर्णन–

CHART - ________

DESCRIPTION
HISTORIQUE ET GÉOGRAPHIQUE
DE L'INDE,

[illegible]

LE PERE JOSEPH TIEFFENTHALER,

[illegible]

M. ANQUETIL DU PERRON,

[illegible]

M. JAQUES RENNELL,

[illegible]

M. JEAN BERNOULLI.

[illegible]

A BERLIN, MDCCLXXXVI.

[illegible]

Important note: Father Joseph Tieffenthaler was an Austrian Jesuit father (1710-1785) who travelled to India in the 1740s and stayed on till his death, adding to his missionary activities a detailed geographical study of the country. His Descriptio Indiae, written in Latin, was translated into French and incorporated in a three-volume series on Indian geography and history published in French from Berlin in 1786.

HISTORICAL EVIDENCE

254 LA PROVINCE D'OUDE

[illegible]

IMPORTANT NOTE

Father Joseph Tieffenthaler was an Austrian Jesuit Father (1710-1785) traveled to India in the 1740 and stayed in India till his death, adding to his missionary activities a detailed geographical study of the country. His Descriptio Indiae, (Historique Et Geographique - DE L') written in Latin, was translated into French and incorporated in three-volume series on India's geography and history published in French from Berlin in 1786.

LA PROVINCE D'OUDE 253

[illegible]

Book - Historique Et Geographique - DE L' Inde

Page 253

Emperor Auranzeb got the fortress called Ramcot demolished and got constructed at the same place, a Mosque with three domes. Some believe that it was constructed by 'Babber'. Fourteen black stone pillars can be seen there, which existed at the site of the fortress.

A square box raised 5 inches above the ground, with borders made of lime, with a length of more than 5 inches and height of about 4 inches can be seen there.

Page 254

THE PROVINCE OF OUDE (UP)

The Hindus call it Bedi i.e. "the cradle". The reason for this is that once upon a time, there was a house in this place where Beschan was born in the from Ram besides his three brothers. Subsequently Aurangzeb or according to another belief, Baber, got this placed destroyed in order to deny from the opportunity of practicing their superstitions. However, there still exists some superstitious cult in some place. For example, in the place where native house of Ram existed, they go around 3 times and prostrate on the floor.

On the 24th of the Tschet month, a big gathering of people gather here to celebrate the birthday of Ram, so famous in entire India.

CHART - 31

HISTORICAL EVIDENCE

A
HISTORICAL SKETCH
OF
TAHSIL FYZABAD, ZILLAH FYZABAD
INCLUDING
PARGANAS HAVELI-OUDH AND PACHHIMRATH,
WITH THE OLD CAPITALS,
AJUDHIA AND FYZABAD,
By P. Carnegy, Officiating Commissioner and Settlement Officer,

PARGANA MANGALSI,
By J. Woodburn, Officiating Settlement Officer,

AND

PARGANA AMSIN
By C. S. Noble, Assistant Settlement Officer,

LUCKNOW
PRINTED AT THE OUDH GOVERNMENT PRESS

1870

A Historical Sketch of Tahsil Fyzabad, Zilah Fyzabad - Including Parganas Haveli-Oudh and Pachhimrath with the old Capitals

AJUDHIA AND FYZABAD
By P Carnegy, Officiating Commissioner and Settlement Officer

PARGANA MANGALSI
By J. Woodburn, Officiating Settlement Officer and

LUCKNOW - 1870
Page 5

PARGANA AMSIN
by C.S. Noble, Assistant Settlement Officer

The restoration by Vikramajit - To him the restoration of the neglected and forest-concealed Ajudhia is universally attributed. His main clue in tracing the ancient city was of course the holy river Sarju, and his next was the shrine still known as Nageshar-nath, which is dedicated to Mahadeo, and which presumably escaped the devastations of the Buddhist and Atheist period. With these clues, and aided by descriptions which he found recorded in ancient manuscripts, the different spots rendered sacred by association with the worldly acts of the deified Rama, were identified, and Vikramajit is said to have indicated the different shrines to which pilgrims from afar still in thousands half-yearly flock.

Page 20 - last para - The Janmasthan and other temples - It is locally affirmed that at the Mahomedan conquest there were three important Hindu shrines, with but few devotees attached, at Ajudhia which was then little other than a wilderness. These were the "Janmasthan" the "Sargadwar mandir" also known as "Ram Darbar", and the "Treta-ke-Thakur".

On the first of these the Emperor Babar built the mosque which still bears his name A.D. 1528. On the second Aurangzeb did the same A.D 1658-1707; and on the third that sovereign, or his predecessor, built a mosque, according to the well known Mahomedan principle of enforcing their religion on all those whom they conquered.

HISTORICAL EVIDENCE

GAZETTEER
OF THE
PROVINCE OF OUDH

VOL. 1.--A. TO G
(THREE VOLS IN ONE)

LOW PRICE PUBLICATIONS
Delhi-110052.

Gazetteer of the Province of Oudh, Vol. 1 - A to G (Three vols in one)

Page No. 6

The Janamasthan and other temples - It is locally affirmed that at the Muhammadan conquest there were three important Hindu shrines, with but few devotees attached, at Ajodhya, which was then little other than a wilderness. These were the "Janamasthan,", the "Swargaddwar mandir" also known as "Ram Darbar,", "Trata-ka-Thakur."

On the first of these the Emperor Babar built the mosque, which still bears his name, A.D.1528. On the 2nd, Aurangzeb did the same, A.D. 1658 to 1707; and on the third, that sovereign or his predecessors built a mosque, according to the well-known Muhammadan principle of enforcing their religion on all those whom they conquered.

The Janamasthan marks the place where Ram Chandar was born. The Swargaddwar is the gate through which he passed into paradise, possibly the spot where his body was burned. The Trata-Ka-Thakur was famous as the place where Rama performed a great sacrifice, and which he commemorated by setting up there images of himself and Sita.

HISTORICAL EVIDENCE

CHART - ______

FYZABAD:

A GAZETTEER

BEING

VOLUME XLII

OF THE

DISTRICT GAZETTEERS OF THE UNITED PROVINCES OF AGRA AND OUDH.

BY

H. R. NEVILL, I. C. S.

ALLAHABAD

PRINTED BY F. LUKER, SUPDT., GOVT. PRESS, UNITED PROVINCES.

1905

Page 173

FYZABAD

A Gazetteer being Volume XLIII of the District Gazetteers of the United Provinces of Agra and Oudh by H.R. Nevill, I.C.S - 1905

It is locally affirmed that at the time of the Musalman conquest there were three important Hindu shrines at Ajodhya and little else. These were the Janamasthan temple, the Swargaddwar, and the Treta-ka-Thakur, and each was successively made the object of attention of different Musalman rulers. The Janamasthan was in Ramkot and marked the birthplace of Rama. In 1528 A.D. Babar came to Ayodhya and halted here for a week. He destroyed the ancient temple and on its site built a mosque, still known as Babar's mosque. The materials of the old structure were largely employed, and many of the columns are in good preservation; they are of close-grained black stone, called by the natives kasauti, and carved with various devices.

HISTORICAL EVIDENCE

CHART - 34

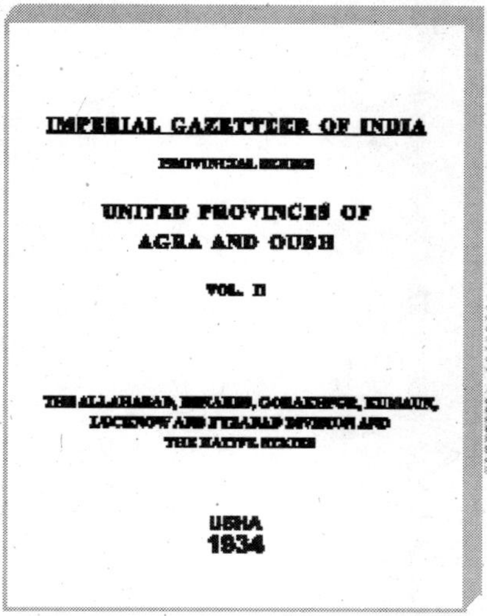

IMPERIAL GAZETTEER OF INDIA

PROVINCIAL SERIES

UNITED PROVINCES OF AGRA AND OUDH

VOL. II

THE ALLAHABAD, BENARES, GORAKHPUR, KUMAUN, LUCKNOW AND FYZABAD DIVISIONS AND THE NATIVE STATES

USHA
1934

Page - 389

Imperial Gazetteer of India, -- Provincial series -
United Provinces of Agra & Oudh - Vol. II - 1934 -

The present town stretche inland from a high bluff overlooking the Gogra. At one corner of a vast mound known as Ramkot, or the fort of Rama, is the holy spot where the hero was born. Most of the enclosure is occupied by a mosque built by Babar from the remains of an old temple, and in the outer portion a small platform and shrine mark the birthplace. Close by is a larger temple in which is shown the cooking place of Sita, the faithful wife of Rama.

CHART - ....

HISTORICAL EVIDENCE

LUCKNOW ARM

VOL IX JULY 1936 PART II

THE JOURNAL OF THE UNITED PROVINCES HISTORICAL SOCIETY

CONTENTS

BABUR AND THE HINDUS

alternative was not palatable to Vikramaditya both because of the distance of the jagir from Rajputana and its comparatively moist climate. So the whole proposal fell through. But Babur's tact may be seen from the following facts:—

(1) He permitted Vikramaditya not to insist on his demand of Biana but to give a consideration to Babur's alternative.

(2) Babur allowed Hindu envoys to negotiate for both the parties, his representative being Hemraj, son of Dewa of Bhira. Dewa has been already mentioned as envoy from Daulat Khan's son, Ali Khan, in 1519. He had transferred his services, later on, to Babur and the latter, finding him intelligent and loyal, utilised him on other diplomatic or political occasions.

The Jami Masjid at Ajodhya.

The present *Jami Masjid* at Ajodhya was built in Babur's time on a site sacred to the Hindus as Rama's birth-place. It is a spacious building with a magnificent hall and massive walls. It has two inscriptions which have supplied us with the date of its building and the name of the builder.

The inscription inside the mosque reads as follows:—

Translation

(1) By the Command of the Emperor Babur, whose justice is an edifice reaching the very height of the heaven

Lucknow Arm -Vol. IX - July 1936 Part II

The Journal of the United Provinces Historical Society

Page 76 - para 3

The Jami Masjit at Ajodhya

The present Jami Masjid at Ajodhya was built in Babur's time on a site sacred to the Hindus as Rama's birth-place. It is a spacious building with a magnificent hall and massive walls. It has two inscriptions which have supplied us with the date of its building and the name of the builder.

The inscription inside the mosque reads as follows:

Panel (Persian) ....

Translation

1. By the command of the Emperor Babur, whose justice is an edifice reaching the very height of the heaven

2. The good hearted Mir Baqi built this alighting place of the angels.

3. May this goodness last for ever. The year of building was made clear likewise, when I said "Buad Khair baqi"

Annexure 4

61

SITE AFTER EXCAVATION-2003

उत्खनन के बाद स्थान

62
FOUND IN EXCAVATION-2003
उत्खनन से प्राप्त अवशेष

FOUND IN EXCAVATION-2003
उत्खनन से प्राप्त अवशेष

64
FOUND IN EXCAVATION-2003
उत्खनन से प्राप्त अवशेष

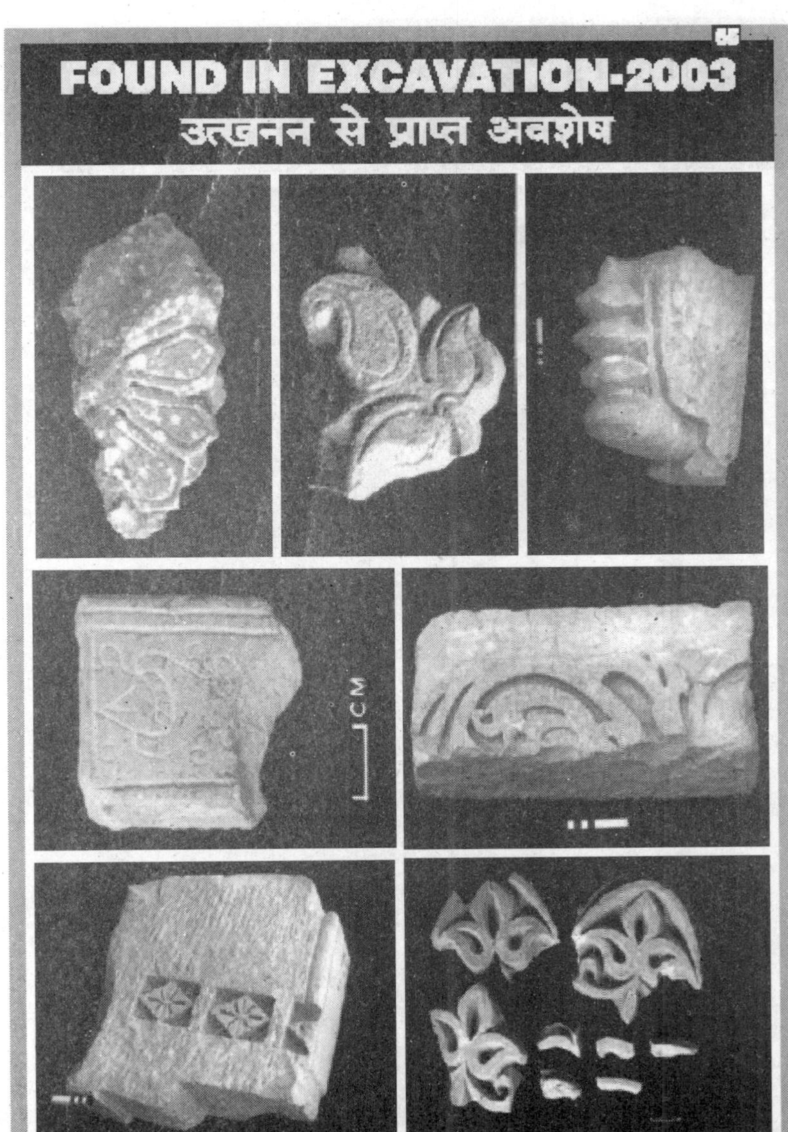
FOUND IN EXCAVATION-2003
उत्खनन से प्राप्त अवशेष
CM

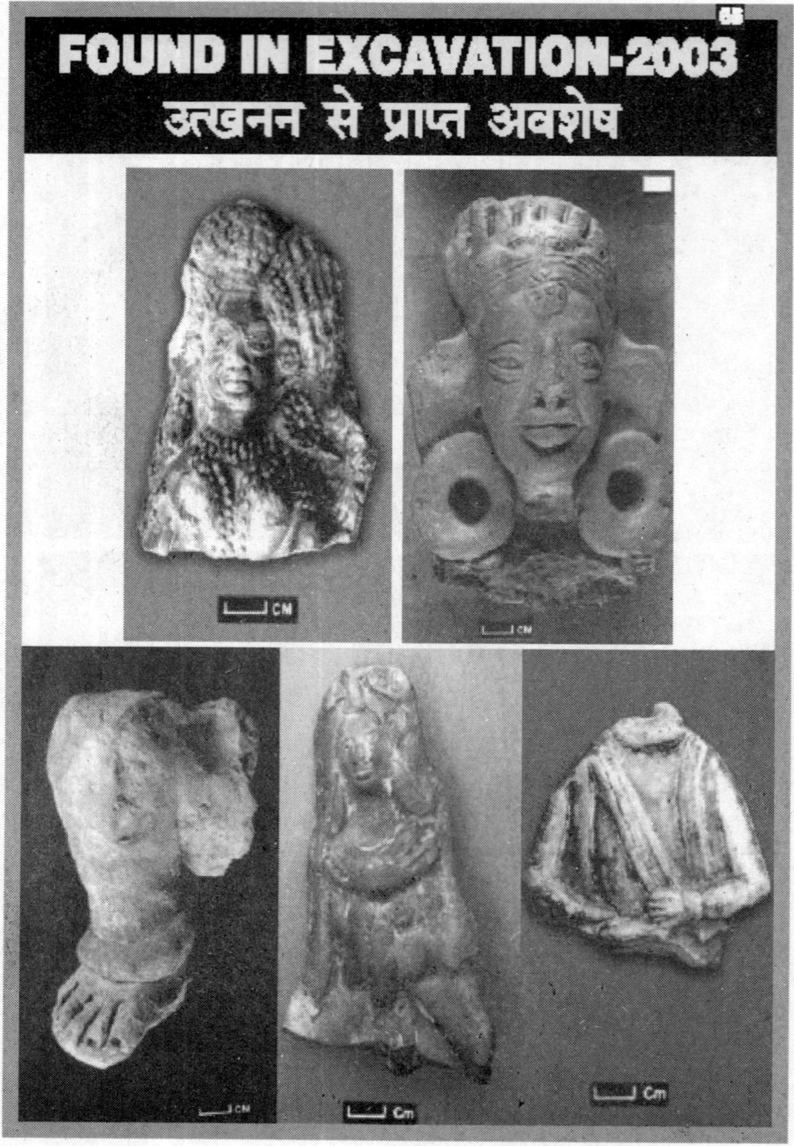
FOUND IN EXCAVATION-2003
उत्खनन से प्राप्त अवशेष
CM
CM
CM
Cm
Cm

THE

RÁMÁYAN OF VÁLMÍKI

TRANSLATED INTO ENGLISH VERSE

BY

RALPH T. H. GRIFFITH, M.A., C.I.E.

FORMER PRINCIPAL OF THE BENARES COLLEGE, AND LATE DIRECTOR
PUBLIC INSTRUCTION N.-W. P. AND OUDH.

COMPLETE IN ONE VOLUME.

BENARES:
PRINTED AND PUBLISHED BY E. J. LAZARUS AND CO.
SOLD ALSO BY
LUZAC AND CO., LONDON.

1895.

5. There is no certain testimony for an epic Mahābhārata before the 4th century B. C.

6. Between the 4th century B. C. and the 4th century A. D. the transformation of the *epic* Mahābhārata into our present compilation took place, probably gradually.

7. In the 4th century A. D. the work already had, on the whole, its present extent, contents and character.

8. Small alterations and additions still continued to be made, however, even in later centuries.

9. *One* date of the Mahābhārata does not exist at all, but the date of every part must be determined on its own account.

The Rāmāyaṇa, both a Popular Epic and an Ornate Poem.

(The Rāmāyaṇa differs essentially from the Mahābhārata in more respects than one.) (Above all it is much shorter and of much greater uniformity.) (While the Mahābhārata in its present form can scarcely be called an actual epic, the Rāmāyaṇa, even in the form in which we have it to-day, is still a fairly unified heroic poem.) Moreover, while (indigenous tradition) names Vyāsa, an entirely mythical seer of ancient times, who was supposed to be at the same time the compiler of the Vedas and of the Purāṇas, as the author or editor of the Mahābhārata, it attributes the authorship of the Rāmāyaṇa to a poet named Vālmīki, and we have no reason to doubt that a poet of this name really lived and first shaped the ballads, which were scattered in the mouths of the bards, into the form of a unified poem. The Indians call this Vālmīki "the first Kavi or author of ornate poetry" (*ādikavi*) and like to call the Rāmāyaṇa "the first ornate poem" (ādikāvya). The beginnings of ornate epic poetry do indeed lead back to the Rāmāyaṇa, and Vālmīki has always remained the pattern to which all later Indian poets admiringly aspired.) The essential factor of Indian ornate poetry, of the so-called "*kāvya*," is that greater importance is attached to the form than to the matter and contents of the poem, and that so-called *alaṃkāras, i.e.* "embellishments," such as similes, poetic figures, puns, and so on, are used largely, even to excess. Similes are heaped on similes, and descriptions, especially of nature, are spun out interminably with ever new metaphors and comparisons. (We find the first beginnings of these and other peculiarities of the classical ornate poetry in the Rāmāyaṇa. While we found in the Mahābhārata a mixture of popular epic and theological didactic poetry (purāṇa), the Rāmāyaṇa appears to us as a work that is popular epic and ornate poetry at the same time.)

(It is a true popular epic, just like the Mahābhārata, because, like the latter, it has become the property of the whole Indian people and, as scarcely any other poem in the entire literature of the world, has influenced the thought and poetry of the nation for centuries.) In the introduction to the epic (a later addition) it is related that god Brahman himself invited the poet Vālmīki to glorify the deeds of Rāma in verse; and the god is said to have promised him:

> "As long as in this firm-set land
> The streams shall flow, the mountains stand,
> So long throughout the world, be sure,
> The great Rāmāyan shall endure."[1]

This dictum has proved itself truly prophetic to the present day. (Since more than two thousand years the poem of Rāma has kept alive in India, and it continues to live in all grades and classes of the people. High and low, prince and peasant, nobleman, merchant and artisan, princesses and shepherdesses, all are quite familiar with the characters and

---

[1]) I, 2, 36 f. Translated by R. T. H. *Griffith.*

THIRD SERIES · VOLUME 29 · PART 4
OCTOBER · 2019

Journal of the Royal Asiatic Society

CAMBRIDGE
UNIVERSITY PRESS

ISSN: 1356-1863

Photograph of Baburi mosque and Ram's birthplace from P. Carnegy's book

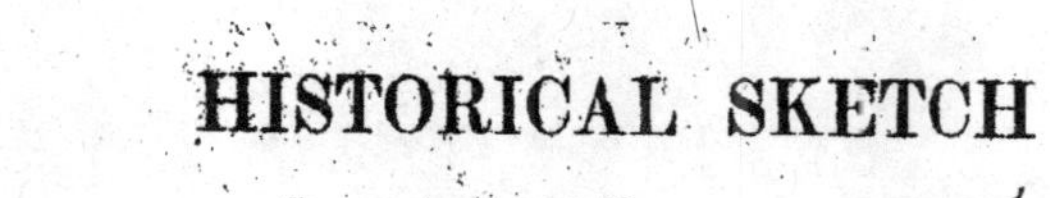

HISTORICAL SKETCH

OF

TAHSIL FYZABAD, ZILLAH FYZABAD,

INCLUDING

PARGANAS HAVELI-OUDH AND PACHHIMRATH,

WITH THE OLD CAPITALS

AJUDHIA AND FYZABAD,

By P. Carnegy, Officiating Commissioner and Settlement Officer.

PARGANA MANGALSI,

By J. Woodburn, Officiating Settlement Officer.

AND

PARGANA AMSIN.

By C. S. Noble, Assistant Settlement Officer.

LUCKNOW.

PRINTED AT THE OUDH GOVERNMENT PRESS.

1870.

Photograph of Baburi mosque and Ram's birthplace from P. Carnegy's book

BÁBAR'S MOSQUE AND RAMA'S BIRTH PLACE

Photograph of Baburi mosque and Ram's birthplace from P. Carnegy's book

HISTORICAL SKETCH

OF

TAHSIL FYZABAD, ZILLAH FYZABAD,

INCLUDING

PARGANAS HAVELI-OUDH AND PACHHIMRATH,

WITH THE OLD CAPITALS

AJUDHIA AND FYZABAD,

By P. Carnegy, Officiating Commissioner and Settlement Officer.

PARGANA MANGALSI,

By J. Woodburn, Officiating Settlement Officer.

AND

PARGANA AMSIN.

By C. S. Noble, Assistant Settlement Officer.

LUCKNOW.

PRINTED AT THE OUDH GOVERNMENT PRESS.

1870.

Photograph of Baburi mosque and Ram's birthplace from P. Carnegy's book

BÁBAR'S MOSQUE AND RAMA'S BIRTH PLACE

Relevant extract of "Some Years Travels Into Divers Parts of Africa and Asia the Great" (Thomas Herbert book)

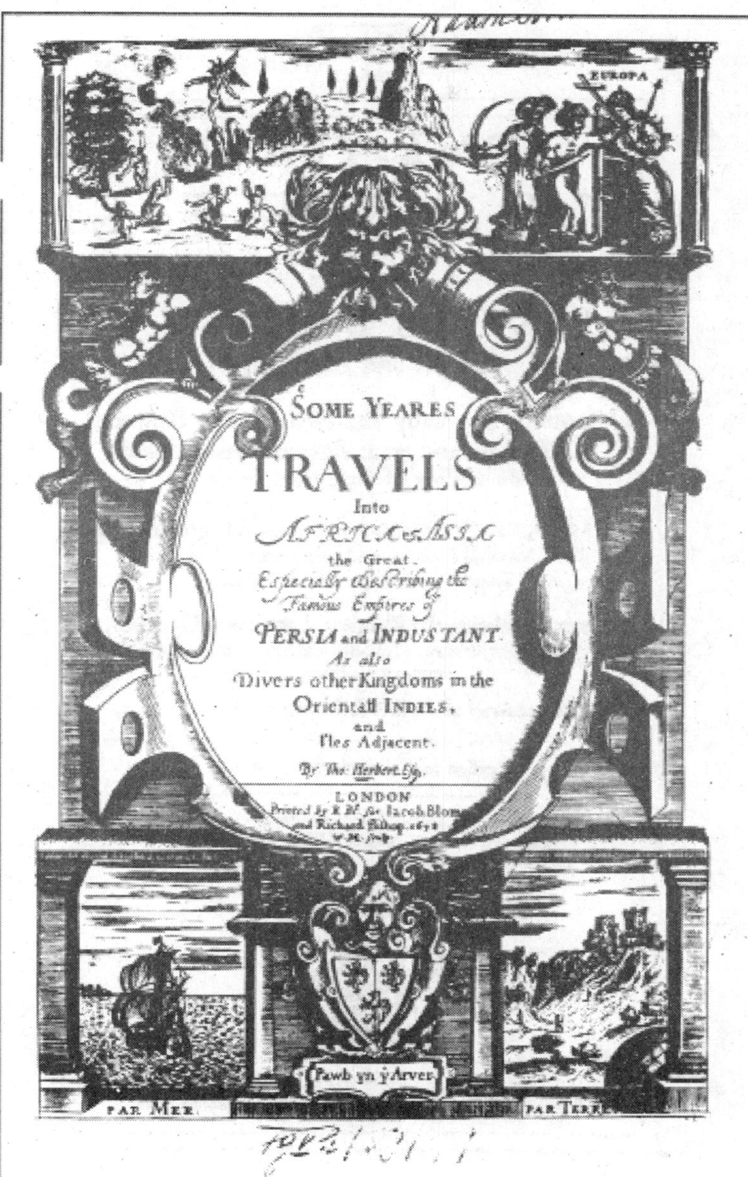

SOME YEARES
TRAVELS
Into
AFRICA & ASIA
the Great.
Especially Describing the
Famous Empires of
PERSIA and INDUSTANT
As also
Divers other Kingdoms in the
Orientall INDIES,
and
Iles Adjacent.
By Tho: Herbert Esq.

LONDON
[illegible]

Relevant extract of "Some Years Travels Into Divers Parts of Africa and Asia the Great" (Thomas Herbert book)

SOME YEARES
TRAVELS
INTO
DIVERS PARTS OF
ASIA and AFRIQUE.

Describing especially the two famous Empires, the *Persian*, and great *Mogull*: weaved with the History of these later Times

As also, many rich and spatious Kingdomes in the Orientall INDIA, and other parts of ASIA; Together with the adjacent Iles.

Severally relating the Religion, Language, Qualities, Customes, Habit, Descent, Fashions, and other Observations touching them.

With a revivall of the first Discoverer of AMERICA.

Revised and Enlarged by the Author.

Segniùs irritant Animos demissa per Aures
Quam quæ sunt Oculis Subjecta fidelibus, & Quæ
Ipse sibi prabet Spectator. Horat.

LONDON,
Printed by R. Bi[illegible] for *Iacob Bloome* and *Richard Bishop*. 1638.

Relevant extract of 'William Finch's account of Oudh'

PVRCHAS
HIS
PILGRIMES.

IN FIVE BOOKES.

The first, Contayning the Voyages and Peregrinations made by *ancient* Kings, *Patriarkes*, Apostles, *Philosophers*, *and* others, to and thorow the remoter parts of the knowne World: *Enquiries also of Languages and Religions, especially of the* moderne diuersified Professions of CHRISTIANITIE.

The second, *A Description of all the Circum-Nauigations* of the GLOBE.

The third, Nauigations and Voyages of *English-men*, alongst the Coasts of Africa, *to the Cape of* Good Hope, *and from thence to the* Red Sea, *the* Abassine, *Arabian*, Persian, *Indian*, Shoares, Continents, and Ilands.

The fourth, English *Voyages beyond the East* Indies, *to the Ilands of* Iapan, *China*, *Cauchinchina*, the *Philippinae* with others, and the *Indian* Nauigations further prosecuted: Their iust Commerce, nobly vindicated against *Turkish* Treacherie; victoriously defended against *Portugall* Hostilitie; *gloriously aduanced against Moorish and Ethnike Perfidie*; hopefully recouering from Dutch Malignitie; iustly maintained against Ignorance and Calumnie.

The fifth, Nauigations, Voyages, Traffiques, Discoueries, of the *English* Nation *in the Easterne parts of the World: continuing the* English-Indian *occurrents*, and contayning the *English* Affaires with the *Great Samorine*, in the *Persian* and *Arabian* Gulfes, and in other places of the Continent, and Ilands of and beyond the Indies: the *Portugall* Attempts, and Dutch Disasters, *diuers Sea-fights with both*; and many other remarkable RELATIONS.

The First Part.

Unus Deus, Una Veritas.

LONDON

Printed by *William Stansby* for *Henrie Fetherstone*, and are to be sold at his shop in *Pauls* Church-yard at the signe of the Rose.

1625.

Joseph Tieffenthaler's account on Ayodhya at Ramajanmabhumi in German language

Des Pater

Joseph Tieffenthaler

d. S. J. und apostol. Mißionarius in Indien

historisch-geographische

Beschreibung von Hindustan.

Aus Dessen lateinischen Handschrift übersetzt.

Mit Anmerkungen und anderen Zusätzen, vorzüglich mit des Engl. Ingenieur-Major Herrn Rennell großen Charte von Hindustan,

herausgegeben

von

Johann Bernoulli,

der Königl. Akademie der Wissenschaften zu Berlin ordentl. Mitgliede und mehr anderen ausserordentl. Mitgliede.

Erster Theil,

welcher Tieffenthalers Beschreibung von Hindustan nebst einer Charte des alten Indien enthält.

Berlin, bey dem Herausgeber

Gotha, bey C. W. Ettinger.

1785.

Relevant extract of "Annual Report of the Office of the Archaeological Surveyor, Northern Circle, Agra"

स्पीड पोस्ट

संख्या: भा0पु0स0/17/सू0/09 | 555
भारत सरकार
भारतीय पुरातत्व सर्वेक्षण
आगरा मण्डल, आगरा।

दिनांक 23 MAY 2011

ी किशोर कुणाल
ायन निलय
[illegible] रोड, [illegible] आश्रम के पास
टना-800010

विषय- सूचना का अधिकार अधिनियम 2005 के अन्तर्गत महानिदेशक कार्यालय, भारतीय पुरातत्व सर्वेक्षण नई दिल्ली को भेजा गया आप का पत्र जो इस कार्यालय में दिनांक 06.05.2011 को प्राप्त हुआ।

महोदय,

आपके उपरोक्त सम्बन्धित पत्र के सम्बन्ध में अवगत कराना है कि पत्र में सन्दर्भित पुस्तक 100 वर्ष से अधिक पुरानी है तथा काफी क्षतिग्रस्त अवस्था में है। तथापि आपके पत्र के अनुसार सम्बन्धित पृष्ठों की छायाप्रति (कुल 2 पृष्ठ) आपके सन्दर्भ हेतु संलग्न की जा रही है।

23/5/11
केन्द्रीय जन सूचना अधिकारी

A photocopy of the exact birthplace of Rama

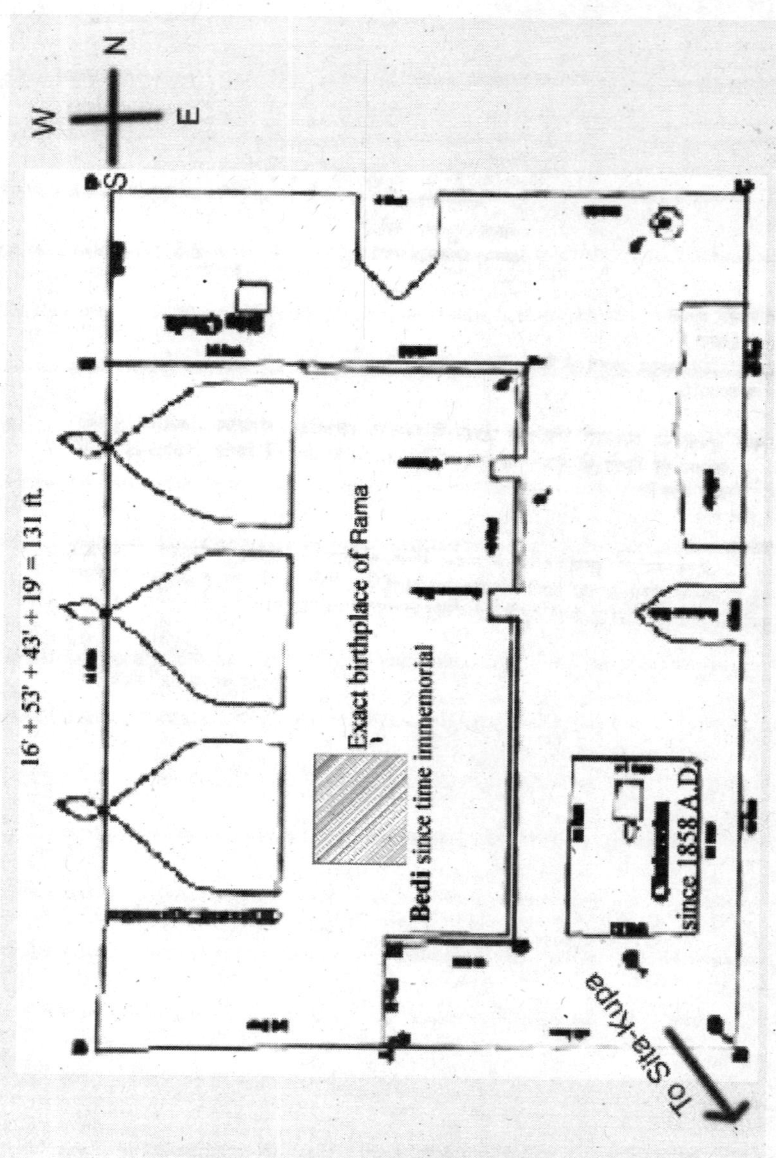

A photograph of Janam Asthan in Tareekh-e-ajoddhiya (1902 A.D.)

تاریخ اجودھیا

جسمین

حالات بابرکات سلطان کومین شہنشاہ و وارین مہاراج [illegible] و

وزیر راجگان و مہاراجگان اجودھیا مندرج ہین

مصنفہ

مسند نشین ایوان ریاست [illegible] دولت و امارت کنور [illegible] صاحب بہادر

تعلقدار ریاست [illegible] علاقہ [illegible] و رئیس اعظم

و آنریری مجسٹریٹ [illegible] متخلص بہ مہر

جسکو

مصنف معزی الیہ نے نہایت توجہات و بخت عرق ریزی سے کتب ہاے معتبر

و نسخہاے معتبرہ سے تحقیق و تصدیق فرما کر جمع کر حالات بچشم دیدہ مدون فرمایا

حسب فرمائش حضرت مصنف معزی الیہ بار اول

مطبع منشی نولکشور واقع لکھنؤ مین طبع ہوئی

۱۹۰۲ء

Bibliography

1. Maurice Winternitz 'A History Indian literature' volume 1 1927 page 476
2. Ralph t h Griffith 'The Ramayan of Valmiki translated into English worse' 1895 page 562
3. F.E. Pargitter article on 'the geography of Rama's exile'.
4. Herbert Thomas, Some Years Travels Into Divers Parts of Asia and Afrique, London 1638.
5. Jain Meenakshi, The India They Saw Vol. III, First Edition 2011, Ocean Books (P)Ltd.
6. Ramaswami Venbakkam Desika, Sri Rama Patha Yathirai, 1973 Sita Rama Bhakta Sabha
7. Report by Montogomery Martin, British Surveyor, 1838.
8. Thornton Edward, East India Company Gazetteer, 1854.
9. Balfour Edward: Encyclopaedia of India and of Eastern and Southern Asia 1858 Edition.
10. Carnegy Patrick : Historical Sketch of Tahsil Fyzabad 1970.
11. Jain Meenakshi, Rama and Ayodhya, first edition 2013, Aryan Books International.
12. Kunal Kishore, Ayodhya : Beyond Adduced Evidence, first edition 2018, Ocean Books (P)Ltd.

13. Kunal Kishore, Ayodhya Revisited, first edition 2016, Ocean Books (P)Ltd.

14. Goel Sita Ram, Hindu Temples: What Happened to Them Vol. I and II.

15. Report of Settlement of the Land Revenue of Fyzabad District by K.F. Mitchell.

16. Allamah Muhammad Najmu, I-Ghani Khan Rampuri, Tarikh-I – Awadh, Vol. V.

17. Sita Ram Lala, Ayodhya ka Itihasa.

18. Jafari Ahmad, Wajid: Alishahaur UnkaAhd, Lucknow: Kitab Manzil 1957.

19. Dutta PrabhashK, Ayodhya: When Mulayam Singh Yadav ordered police firing on Kar Sevaks heading to Babri Masjid, India Today online report ,October 30, 2019.

20. RamJanambhumi Ayodhya: New Archeological Discoveries (NAD; Sharma, Y.D., K.M. Srivastava et al. 1992).

21. Sharma Hemant, YudhmeinAyodhya, first edition 2018, Prabhat Prakashan.

22. Sharma Hemant, Ayodhya Ka Chashmadeed, 2019, Prabhat Paperbacks.

23. Sandipan Deb, Outlook India, June 23, 2003.

24. www.Sandhayajainarchive.org/2003/09/09/ayodhya-lost-and-found

25. www.elegalix.allahabadhighcourt.in/elegalix/ayodhyafiles/honsukj-gist.pdf

26. Stephen Knapp gives a detailed account about historicity of Rama in an article titled, 'Lord Rama: fact or Fiction'.

□□□